A F

Curse

Nat N.W.

DEDICATION

To my loving husband, Nick, for the countless hours helping me sort through and write this book. The journey has been wild but I am thankful to have you alongside through everything

To my friend Dakota Frandsen, for seeing this book, helping work out all the behind the scenes so publication was possible

CONTENTS

Table of Contents

"Chaos: When the present determines the future, but the approximate present does not approximately determine the future"

- Edward Lorenz

ACKNOWLEDGMENTS

Writing a book is a lot harder than I thought. It takes a lot of time to make sure everything is correct. This was my first time writing a book. I never thought I would be capable of writing a book. I majored in Criminal Justice/Criminology and Minored in Psychology. I work full-time as a police dispatcher. I have a great interest in law enforcement, the criminal mind, and mental illness. We are still in the dark ages of mental illness. We don't know as much as we should know. Millions of people suffer from it and are completely isolated in this world. Although this story is fiction, I hope it sparks people's interest in the severity of mental illness and its cause. This story has been on my mind for a long time. I finally got the courage to write it down and share the vision I had when writing this with people.

I would like to say thank you to my husband, Nick. He took more than a tremendous amount of time to do what he could to edit my book, and I could not have done it without him. Thank you so much for all your love and support. You are truly remarkable.

FINALLY, THANK YOU TO EVERYONE WHO READ AND BOUGHT MY BOOK. I HOPE YOU ENJOYED IT. I NEVER THOUGHT I WOULD BE ABLE TO DO THIS, AND I HOPE TO WRITE MORE AND GET BETTER AS I GO ALONG.

A BEAUTIFUL CURSE

My name is Jennifer Bailey. I am fifteen years old and a sophomore at King High School. I wish that I could tell you that I am just an ordinary teenage girl. I cannot distinguish between certain times, places, and people, and I do not have that luxury, at least not anymore. There are only certain times, places, people, sights and smells that stick out most in my mind. They are here for a moment and gone the next. Minor, insignificant occurrences happen to people every day. They fail to take notice, but it's magnified in my eyes. The sun, rain, snow, cold, and heat are heightened.

An average person would not be able to comprehend what happens in my life daily. I can slow things down or speed things up. I can "skip" the parts of my life that I want to skip. The things that I see and hear - the majority of people can only imagine. Most of the time, I am entirely unaware of what is around me until I see it, listen to it, and feel it. That's how I know it's real. That is how anyone would know anything is real. When sights and feelings come across my mind, I try to hold on to them as long as I can because those memories will soon be gone. Just as quick as they came.

One of the things that I am able to hold onto the most are the seasons. Seasons will always be there; nothing can make them go away. No matter where I am in life, I will always be in one of the four seasons. They are the one thing that I can count on to remain consistent in my eyes and life.

Seasons have a special feeling. Winter brings the warmth of being inside on a snowy Christmas day. Spring is when the flowers start to bloom, and school is coming to an end. Summer is pretty self-explanatory. Three months of freedom, warmth, sun, and fun.

Of all of the seasons, fall is my favorite. It is the most memorable. The weather starts to turn cooler, and the rain has a slight chance of turning to snow. The leaves are changing from dark green to yellow, to orange, and to red. The apple cider begins to hit the shelves at the grocery stores, along with the pumpkins and Halloween decorations. Although fall is my favorite season, I have also come to dread it, unfortunately. It comes with my darkest memories, at least the memories that I believe.

It was September 6th. School had been in session for two weeks now, starting on August 23rd. The temperatures dropping for the beginning of

September. I was hoping that it would be a warm September and October, but it was not turning out to be what I had expected. That morning was tough for me to get out of bed. It was foggy and rainy, and the clouds just didn't want to lift. It was the perfect time to sleep in, but I had to get up for school. I dreaded school, especially high school.

I was not popular and did not have many friends. Girls did not talk to me, and boys did not like me because they liked the popular girls. I did not have the self-confidence that the other girls had. I was of average height and average weight. Brown hair and brown eyes. I did not wear makeup and dressed in baggy clothing. Deep down, I always knew I was different. I just didn't know by how much. It was apparent that I did not fit in, though. The popular girls wore makeup and had outrageous outfits, which all the popular guys liked; the complete opposite of who I was. The popular girls were in sports or cheerleading. The popular guys played football.

The thought of spending another day there was unpleasant. I was incensed with dread for some reason. I did not want to get out of bed, but I had to. I managed to drag myself out from under the covers. I put on a hoodie and a pair of jeans and headed out the door.

I usually walked to school because my parents worked, and I did not yet have a driver's license. It was frigid and rainy, and carrying my heavy backpack only made things worse. My hair was getting wet, causing it to frizz more than usual, so I pulled it back and pulled up the hood on my hoodie. The fog and mist were so thick it was hard to see through. However, I could see lights on in the houses as I passed by. There was a dim, glowing warmth to the light. I could sense people's comfort in their homes. Dads and Moms were getting ready for work, and kids were getting ready to go to school. It was not a bad neighborhood; it was what you would call upscale, actually.

I always walk by an elementary school on the way to my high school. Just beyond the elementary school was a gazebo with four benches and a table. There was also a tiny playground meant for small children, judging by the size of the swings. On the other side, a sidewalk leads around the grass and the neighborhoods behind it. The grass had water and what looked like frost on it. There were wet leaves all over the sidewalk.

Something about that morning was different, and I knew it when I woke up and felt that dread.

4

CHAPTER 2
FIRST WALK

As I walked down the wet sidewalk, I kept looking at my feet and looking at the wet leaves that I stepped on as I walked to school. The gazebo was coming up. Behind it was a swing set and playground. It had mulch, not the usual gravel. I looked at the tables and noticed a boy sitting at one of them. He was just staring at the swing set. I could only see the back of him. I didn't know who he was. He was wearing a black jacket and jeans. He had dark brown hair that was a little bit longer than expected. I continued to walk, trying to pretend like I had not noticed him. I picked up my pace as I passed the gazebo, so I didn't have to make eye contact.

However, with my luck, he turned around. I slowed my pace a little bit and then looked directly at him. I did know him or at least knew of him. His name was Derek Kretin, with brown eyes and his hair partly covering his left eye. He looked sad, cold, and damp. I figured he was just on his way to school like I was, but he was just sitting there.

"Hey," he said as I started to walk past him.

I stopped and just looked at him curiously. He stared at me; his eyes were cold and dead. I couldn't help but think that something was wrong.

"Hey, umm, what are you doing?" I asked politely.

Instead of answering, he just continued to look at me with a thousand-mile stare. Ignoring me, as if I was not even there. His hair fell in front of his face, now covering both of his eyes. He was wearing gloves. I guess I could understand, it was getting cold out, and it was raining.

"Derek, what are you doing? Are you going to school?"

He looked down at the ground. Finally, he looked at me again with those icy eyes. It gave me chills. I did not know what to think or say. I walked over to the gazebo and sat at the table across from him. He was still staring at me. No smile, just a straight face, and he looked right into my eyes. His silence was deafening. I knew something was wrong, but what could it be?

"Are you going to school?" I asked again firmly.

"Yeah, I always walk by here on my way. I thought I would just sit for a while." He said uncomfortably, holding his cold stare.

6

I knew Derek was more of an outcast than me, which was saying something. He did not have many friends, and he did not fit into a social group. I saw him a couple of times in the hallway being made fun of by the popular kids, but it never really seemed to bother him. He was an average student, but people did not like him for whatever reason. Although, I was beginning to see why. His demeanor. The mysteriousness. I got up from the table, realizing he was not going to say anything. He watched as I stood up.

"Okay, well, I guess I'll see you at school or something."

He said nothing.

I continued my walk as it started to rain harder, the wind growing intense and cold enough to see my breath.

I reached the school. As I approached, I could hear kids chattering outside. The conversations were so loud, they always echoed. I was just trying to make it to my locker and get to my class on time. I could not stop feeling the dread. Seeing Derek did not help the feeling either. My mind wouldn't stop wandering with the questions that I didn't ask him… *What are you doing here? Is there something wrong? Can I help you? Why are you out here in the rain and cold?*

But I did not ask him. As a matter of fact, I didn't really ask him anything. The day flew by with my five classes. I walked back home the way I had come earlier that morning, right past the gazebo where I ran into Derek, and he wasn't there this time.

I returned to my house, which was not far from the Elementary School. I could smell dinner cooking. Mom gave her usual greeting and said dinner would be ready soon. I thanked her and headed for my room. She would usually ask how my day was and how I was feeling, and I always felt fine. Today, dad came up shortly after and asked the exact same thing. *Odd.*

After doing some homework, I came downstairs and sat on the couch. The house always smelled amazing, especially with the fall candles my mom always had lit. The air smelled of apple cider and spiced pumpkin, along with dinner cooking. It was very comforting, and I felt very content, as it was my safe place.

I ate dinner with my family, we talked about our day. After dinner, I headed back upstairs to finish my homework. I never usually spoke to anyone else because I did not have many friends. I did have Lacy, who was a little bit better at talking to people than I was, but needless to say, she and I were really close. Lacy was like me; average height, skinny, brown hair, and brown eyes. She, too, was a bit of a tomboy. I did not call her that night, and she did not call me. It was fine. We are not the type of friends that need to call each other every single night. I knew I would talk to her in a couple of days, and we would pick up right where we left off.

I was starting to get tired and decided to go to bed.

8

That's when I heard a knock on my door. My sister, Jordan, walked in. She and I were pretty close. She was three years younger than me. Jordan was the complete opposite of me. Unlike myself, she cared about how she looked and how many friends she had. Jordan went to Eagle Middle school, which was not far from King High School. Jordan was beautiful. She was of average height, skinny, with long brown hair and brown eyes. Jordan wore trendy clothes and makeup every day. She was popular at her school. All the girls practically obsessed over her, and all the boys were practically drooling at the chance to date her. Jordan would go out on the weekends with all her friends. It was scarce that her phone did not ring or have an extraordinary amount of incoming texts. I did not envy her social status, but I always wondered how different my life would be if I were like her.

"Hey Jenn, are you doing okay?" Jordan asked, standing at the door.

"Yeah, I'm fine. Why does everyone keep asking me how I am doing? I am the same as I have always been. No offense or anything."

"I am just asking. You're my sister, and I want to know everything is okay with you."

"Well, it is. I am just tired and trying to get homework done."

"Okay, well, then I will just see you tomorrow. Let me know if you want to talk about anything."

"Okay." I looked at her with confusion.

I decided to go to bed. I had a hard time sleeping. I tossed and turned. I could not help thinking about Derek, and I did not know why. I stared at the ceiling most of the night.

"What are you doing?"

"Why are you even talking to me?" Derek asked.

"You seem like you need something or someone to talk to."

"Well, I don't, and you can't fix anything."

"Fix anything? What would I want to fix?" I asked.

"You're seriously going to ask that?" Derek stammered.

"I'm listening, Derek; what is your deal?"

Derek just smiled and didn't say anything more. I looked at him, demanding an answer.

"I'm not going to give you what you want, and I can't!" Derek shouted.

"I don't want anything!" I shouted back.

I woke up. I was still staring at the ceiling. I looked at the clock to see it was midnight. I thought I had been dreaming. I looked around and felt myself dripping in sweat. I did not understand what was going on. I told myself, *'I must have been telling my side of the story.'*

The conversation would have likely sounded like that had I asked Derek all of the questions I wanted to but had not. I tried to fall back asleep, but it was hard. I was confused and uptight for a reason I could not figure out.

The next time I looked at my clock, it was 6 in the morning. I got out of bed in a hurry and began to get dressed. It was Friday, which was not a complete sorrow and dread for the day. I could not stop thinking about the dream. It almost felt like it was not a dream at all, and it felt so real.

I threw on the usual ensemble that I always wore. I wore my dark brown hair down and straight, like always. No makeup. I opened up my shades and noticed it was very foggy, but it wasn't raining. Another perfect excuse to wear a hoodie. I put the hood up and walked out of my bedroom.

As I walked down the stairs, I saw my mom and sister in the kitchen, and they were already drinking coffee. My sister looked great, as usual, and my mom was still in her robe. They both just looked at me as I started for the door.

"Hey Jenn, do you want any coffee or breakfast before you go?" Mom asked, standing with the coffee pot in the kitchen.

"Oh, hey. No, thank you. I will just grab something at school," I said, walking towards the front door. I looked back to see they were staring at each other very oddly. Then they looked back at me. I turned away quickly, opened the front door, and walked outside.

CHAPTER 3
DEREK

The instant I walked out the door, the cold and damp hit me. It was foggy again. As I walked, I looked at the houses surrounding me with the lights shining through the fog. The streets, the sidewalks, and the grass were starting to accumulate more leaves as fall drew nearer.

I thought about what I would say to Derek if I were to walk past him again. I was going to walk past the same pavilion and playground, but I was looking forward to it in a way. I was starting to get anxious to get there. I began to walk at a faster pace than usual.

I could see the gazebo through the fog. The swings were swaying in the wind. I thought I could see someone sitting at the table in the pavilion, but I could not tell for how thick the mists had become. As I got closer, there was someone there. I saw that same black jacket, gloves, and jeans as yesterday. I saw Derek sitting at the table once again. I practically jogged as I moved closer to sit down across from him. He looked up at me slowly, again not saying anything.

"Are you going to make this a regular thing?" I asked.

"What?" Derek asked as he looked up at me.

"You, just sitting here at this table every time I walk by to school."

"Is it wrong to sit here?" Derek looked at me, confused.

"No, but, weirdly, you're sitting here outside in the cold, and it's not exactly nice weather out or anything."

"It's just strange you're even talking to me," he stared at me with his icy eyes.

"Why wouldn't I talk to you? You're sitting right here, and I know who you are."

"Most people don't know me." He looked down again.

"Well, I do. You go to my school, and I see you in the hallways all the time."

"Yeah, keep telling yourself that." He scoffed.

"What is that supposed to mean?" I crossed my arms.

Again, no reply. A man and his dog walked by on the path that passes the gazebo. I looked up and smiled, and he smiled back at me but did not seem to take notice of Derek. I tried to continue the conversation.

14

"So, what is that supposed to mean?" I asked once again.

"I hate school." He said.

"Well, I do too. I mean, look at me. I don't have any friends, and I am not popular or pretty," pointing to my face and clothes.

"Yeah, that's probably why I can talk to you," Derek interrupted.

"You can talk to anyone. You just choose not to." I said firmly.

"That is not the point. I can talk to you and only you." Derek said, looking directly at me.

"Why is that?" I asked.

Derek said nothing. He continued to sit there and stare, here but not really, here.

"I have done some bad things, and I can't explain it," Derek said.

I just stared at him blankly. What could he have possibly done that was so bad?

"Its things that you wouldn't understand and never will understand. Only I can understand because no one else thinks the way I do. Not my parents or my brother. I would say friends, too. Let's face it, though. I don't have any." Derek said.

"I am pretty sure I can understand perfectly because no one understands me either. I want them to

15

understand or just accept me. Be friends with me, but I don't think that is going to happen." I answered back.

"Why not?" Derek asked.

"Because it's just not that way for me. I am too different than what most people can comprehend these days. I will never be on that 'popular kid' level, and it's just not going to happen for me."

"Well, it's definitely not going to happen for me either. I am not going to have any friends, and I will never have friends. I am pretty much stuck," Derek said as he leaned back on the bench of the table.

"You're not stuck, and you're just lost!" I told him, "I guess I can say the same thing about myself."

"You're not stuck. You have your life ahead of you, and you have college and, maybe, someday a career. Not like me." Derek said.

"You can have that too. You are smart and can be motivated, sometimes, but you're not stuck. There is opportunity out there for you."

"There really isn't, though. My decision is final. How can you not see that?" Derek asked.

"What decision? You're seventeen years old. Did you already make a huge decision that you haven't disclosed or something?" I asked, shaking my head.

Derek stopped talking. He started to look at the ground again. I stared back at him. Furthermore, his silence was deafening. I felt like I was precisely where in the world I was supposed to be at that moment. Derek was not telling me anything, and I knew it right away. I was a timid person that kept to myself.

For me to even be having this conversation with him was a huge step. I gave in and picked up his gloved hand. I noticed it was freezing, even with the glove on. He pulled away immediately. I just looked back at him. I knew it was cold out. *How long has he been out here?* The wind was starting to pick up again, and to no surprise, it began to rain.

"Maybe you should just go," Derek said quickly.

"Okay, will you be here tomorrow?" I asked.

"Maybe. I don't know. I just know that I can talk to you." Derek said.

"Do you even know my name?" I asked.

Derek just looked at me with that blank stare, his hair covering his left eye. He gave me a grin. He may not have said anything, but his look suggested he knew who I was. I also felt a sense of hope and consistency from him, which I do not have in my life.

"Well, I have a doctor's appointment tomorrow, but after that, I can come and talk to you. Will you be here? Or at your house? You don't live too far away from here, right?" I asked.

"No, it's not far away, but you can meet me here," Derek said.

"Okay, then I will see you tomorrow. Same gazebo, same bench, I guess," I suggested, shrugging my shoulders.

I stood up and walked away. I looked back to see that Derek was still sitting there, watching me. This time, the pace was slower going to school as I still had so many questions. It dawned on me why Derek was not going to school, and he *had done something*...

I brushed it off. Maybe Derek was just ditching? Of course, I couldn't blame him, given his social status. I reached the school, I could hear the same chit-chat that I continuously hear. I could not understand the conversations around me. Does not matter; I knew I was not a part of them. It was all just noise. A loud, crowded cafeteria.

My first period was Biology. Not like it mattered as I could not pay much attention because everything was running through my mind about Derek. I could not seem to get him out of my head. I still had not seen my friend, Lacy, either. She never texts me back, which is not out of the ordinary for our friendship. However, even this length of time is weird.

Just as soon as school began, it ended. I remember going by my locker and gathering all the stuff that I needed for each class, but it was all a big blur from there. My last class was social studies, and we were on the topic of world history, of which I had very little interest. The bell rang, and we all got up from our desks and started towards the hallway.

All classes had ended. I started to walk down the

hallway. I always looked at my feet as I walked so I did not have to make eye contact with anyone. I went to my locker and took what I needed from it. I started towards the front door of the school. As I walked, my thoughts wandered off to Derek again. *It is Friday, great! Now, I have the entire weekend to wonder why he has suddenly been at the playground.*

I stepped out of the school. I looked around at all of the other kids talking about their plans for the weekend. The parties they were going to go to. I just walked past them, like I usually do, and started on my way home. The walk towards the elementary school seemed longer than it had been. As I looked up, the playground came into sight. I looked at the elementary school; kids were leaving in the distance. I made my way towards the playground and the pavilion.

To my surprise, Derek was not there. I actually began to look for him, but it was useless. The playground was pretty open. Not many places to hide. I gave a heavy sigh and started back for the sidewalk, making my way home.

CHAPTER 4
LET DOWN

The fog had not lifted, and it was still raining for the walk home. There was an ominous feeling in the air. More than the typical gloom that comes with rain and fog-filled day. I opened the front door. The conversation between my Mom and I was about my doctor's appointment in the morning. Afterward, I went to my room and changed into my usual ensemble of hoodies and sweats.

I came back downstairs. Mom had dinner almost ready. She, again, asked me how I was feeling and if everything was okay. My answer was the same as always. I was fine. My sister kept staring at me oddly as we sat through dinner, and I just brushed it off. She was still dressed up in the same clothes she went to school in. I could not understand why she felt the need to always look good, even at home.

I finished with dinner, took my plate to the sink, and started towards the stairs. My mom stopped me and told me to be ready for my doctor's appointment tomorrow. I nodded at her and continued up the stairs into my room.

I did not feel like doing homework, so I just laid on my bed thinking about Derek. I kept thinking about all the weird things he was saying to me. The short answers. His curious, dark demeanor.

I started to fall asleep. I did not have any dreams, or, at least, any that I can remember. I slept through the night, which was surprising.

CHAPTER 5
CRAZY

My mom came in to wake me for my Doctor's appointment. I rubbed my eyes as I sat up in bed. I looked at the clock. 8 in the morning. I slowly started to get up and get dressed. As usual, I threw on jeans and a hoodie. I worked my way down the stairs to find my mom ready to go. We walked towards the garage door. I got into my mom's car, and we started driving to my appointment.

For the majority of the drive, I stared out of the window, wondering if Derek was at the pavilion waiting for me. We drove by my high school, and I watched it with dread. I put my head on the window, waiting to arrive at the Doctor's. We had a brief conversation on the way.

We finally arrived at the Doctor's office, which was only about fifteen minutes away. My mom parked the car, and I got out. We started for the front door of a relatively small office building, and there is an emergency room right next door. On the front of the building is a sign that reads Columbia Medical Center. We walked into the building.

22

Doctor Flora was on the third floor. The third floor was the psychiatric floor. I usually saw the same patients in the waiting room every time I went for my appointments. We waited for what seemed like forever. The nurse finally called me back. My mom stayed in the waiting room.

Doctor Flora walked in and began to assess me.

He asked the usual questions.

"How are you feeling today?" Doctor Flora asked.

"I feel fine. Everything is fine, and I am carrying on like normal." I said.

"Good. So you're not feeling depressed or overwhelmed with anxiety?" the Doctor asked.

"No, I am fine; I just need a refill on my medications because I am out of them and have been for the past five days."

"Right, I will get right on that. How are you feeling about everything that has been going on? Nothing unusual?"

"No. Every morning I walk to school, I have been talking to a guy that I cross paths with every once in a while," I said, nodding my head.

"Which guy?" Doctor Flora asked.

"His name is Derek, he goes to my school, and I have been talking to him a lot lately, well, for the past two days at least."

23

"Oh really? I see, and what does he have to say?" Doctor Flora asked as he crossed his hands on his legs.

"Nothing unusual, really. He's just a social outcast, which is why a lot of people don't talk to him." I answered.

"Nobody should be talking to him." Doctor Flora said, looking directly at me.

"He's not a bad guy, and I think he just needs someone to talk to."

"Okay, well, I am going to up the dose a little more for your medication, and we will just go from there. Does that sound okay?" Doctor Flora said rhetorically.

I just nodded my head and agreed with him. I took the prescription and walked out. My mom was sitting out in the waiting room. Doctor Flora wanted to speak to her privately, and I did not overthink it. I sat in the waiting room and waited for my mom to come out. As she did, I got up and asked her how everything went. She didn't say much, just smiled as if everything was fine.

"Okay, are you ready to go home?" my mom asked.

"Yeah, I'm good," I answered as I stood up from the chair.

We got into her tiny black SUV and began to drive. She said nothing, and neither did I. I put my head back on the window and looked at the trees as the leaves had turned to such beautiful colors. I really love this time of year; it makes me feel so warm and at ease. People were walking with their families, kids, and dogs.

Some were wearing light jackets instead of short sleeve shirts because the weather was beginning to change. As we pulled into our neighborhood, I could see our house. The leaves were everywhere in the street, but the Aspen trees in front of our house still had their leaves. We pulled into the garage, and I got out.

I walked into the house and could see my sister sitting on the couch enjoying her Saturday, watching TV. She looked at me and asked me how I was feeling, but nothing after that. I started to walk upstairs to my room and just sat on my bed. I began to stare at the wall, with my mind starting to go blank. I put my medications on the desk. I realized that I was supposed to meet Derek. I quickly threw on a hoodie, went downstairs, and headed out the door.

CHAPTER 6
TRUE LIES

I took the usual route towards school. Except for this time, I wasn't going to school. I almost wanted to jog just to get there faster, but I didn't because I didn't want to seem desperate to see Derek. My pace towards the school was faster than usual. I caught a visual of the elementary school and continued to walk past the school and the baseball fields. I started on the sidewalk towards the gazebo. I noticed the weather was cloudy, but the sun was beginning to come through this time. More than it had in the past couple of days, which was nice. It was still chilly, though. Fall was not taking its time getting here.

The gazebo finally came into sight, and I could not see anyone. I walked closer and still, could not see anyone. Finally, I got to the point where I could see the pavilion and the tables, but no one was there. I looked at my phone and saw that it was 11:30. Derek and I did not specify a time, but I figured he would be here. I started to walk towards the swing set; my feet were sinking into the mulch since it had been raining. I pushed the swing, and it made a squeaky sound. It made me smile. I sat down at one of the tables under the gazebo to wait for Derek, but as I turned around, there he was.

"Jesus! You scared the hell out of me! What are you doing?" I exclaimed.

"Nothing, just waiting for you to arrive," Derek said.

"I've been here for about ten minutes, and you weren't here," I said, still trying to catch my breath.

"I have been here. This is where we said we would meet, so I am here." Derek said back.

"Yeah, okay, you weren't here. I know that. I sat down at this table, and you weren't here. Did you just show up? Because if so, I didn't hear you."

"No, I have been here. I was just waiting for you." Derek said.

"Okay. Whatever. So let's pick up where you left off. You said you have done some bad things, and I can't change them, or you, for that matter? Does that ring a bell?" I asked, standing crossing my arms.

"I feel like I can talk to you, but I just don't know how I can talk to you. It's not possible, and you can't be here." Derek explained.

"Yeah, well, I am here, and I am talking to you. Explain to me how that is not possible because it's happening right now at this moment." I said, frustrated.

27

Derek said nothing and just kept staring at me as if he knew something that I did not. Which, at that moment, I had no idea what I was supposed to know or what I should know.

"Listen, in the past couple of days, I have really started to like you. You are amazing, and I feel like I can talk to you about anything, but I know you don't like me." Derek said.

"I like you, but Derek, no offense, you force people away from you. People have no choice but to not like you; you're mysterious, dark, and morbidly at that. You're not exactly a 'social' or 'fun' human being. It's not really cool to like a person like you if I am being sincere," I said as I sat in front of him.

"How would you know what's cool and fun? From what I remember, you're not a popular high school cheerleader or into sports. Is that what you want? To fit in so badly that you care about who you talk to and who people see you talking to build up your status, from, I don't know, basically nothing?" Derek said back.

I looked back at him, angry and frustrated. I shook my head and then looked away. Deep down, I knew he was right. I cared about what people thought of me and who I associated with, but in the end, it would not make a difference. I was still made fun of and did not have any friends. It did not matter who I talked to. My social status was made up in the popular kid's minds if they even knew I existed.

I got up from the table and sat on the swing. It was

28

tiny, but I made myself fit. I started to sway in the swing. I looked up to see Derek walking toward me. He, again, was looking at me with cold eyes; standing over me with his hair was falling over his eyes. He was wearing his black jacket, blue jeans, and gloves.

"I am going to do something, and you're not going to be able to stop me. I wasn't fit for this life, and I never will fit in in this life. I have no future, no compassion, no mercy, no sympathy, and no remorse. I don't care what happens to people and the pain that I cause. It doesn't matter anymore. My life doesn't matter anymore. My brain was not fit for this world and society, and I know that. There's nothing here for me. Nobody thinks the way I do, and it's far too complex for anyone to understand. I will make people understand and, maybe, they will see a glimpse of my life.

"It is painful and dreadful to wake up every day with no ambition and no sense of self-preservation. Nobody will forget the day, and that is how I will leave it and leave you. I still can't believe that I am talking to you. I don't know how possible, but this is what it is, and no one will stop me. This needs to happen. Not only for everyone in the world but for you."

I sat there in shock, my eyes wide open. This is the longest I have ever heard Derek talk. I could not believe what he was saying to me. I did not know what to say back, and I felt the same thing. I also thought that I was different and did not belong in this world. Nothing really mattered, but for some reason, I kept finding a way to push on. If I could find a way, then why couldn't Derek?

I looked up at Derek with tears in my eyes. I did not know why I wanted to cry, but I did. I did not let myself cry. I just held it in and pretended to be strong. It seemed like we had been staring at each other forever.

I stood up from the swing. The wind started to pick up, it was getting colder, but I noticed how hard it was around Derek. I reached my hand for him, but he pulled away again. Derek turned away. I grabbed his hand and held on to it. He then turned around and looked right into my eyes. His eyes were still cold. He started to lean in as if to kiss me. I stood there and closed my eyes, waiting for it. I knew I was not going to stop him if he did. He leaned in close enough to kiss me, and I thought I kissed back.

As soon as I opened my eyes, Derek was walking away. He was walking down the sidewalk towards the school. He turned left on the sidewalk, away from the school, and walked. I could see his hair flying back with the wind. It took me a minute to realize what had happened, and I began to follow him. I took the same path and turned left into the neighborhood. I caught a glimpse of his black jacket when I looked right.

I ran towards the house he went into. I was at the front porch. I looked around, but I couldn't find him. I was trying to catch my breath, not realizing I had been running after him. I looked around. There were people walking by and cars driving down the street, and they did not seem to pay much attention to me. I sat outside the house for about ten minutes, not knowing what to do. The thought had occurred to me to just go home and let it go. Let Derek go.

Finally, I got enough courage to walk up to the front door and rang the doorbell. I looked around the house. The lights were on the inside. The door had a customized knocker that read, "The Kretins." This was the right house. No one was answering, so I started to leave. When I reached the end of the stairs to the porch, I decided to turn around and head back to the front door. I rang the doorbell again. I waited for what seemed like forever. Finally, Derek's dad came to the door.

"Hi, Mr. Kretin. I wanted to speak with Derek, please." I said nervously.

"You want to speak with Derek?" Mr. Kretin asked.

"Yes, please. I know he lives here and just wanted to talk to him for a minute," I pleaded.

"Listen, I don't know what you want or why you have come, but this is just not the time. I can't handle any more people coming to my door and property wanting to speak about Derek," he raised his voice towards me.

"What? No, I just wanted to speak with him! He knows me! My name is Jennifer; Derek and I go to the same school! He will want to speak with me," I explained, trying to look past Derek's dad.

"Listen, you might be some sort of acquaintance of Derek, but that doesn't mean you know him, and I

31

will not speak to you about him. I don't care who you are," he continued to raise his voice.

I stood at the front porch and gave Mr. Kretin a perplexed look.

"Please just go home, okay? I can't do this anymore," he said as he shut the door in my face. I stood there staring at the door. I realized I had no choice but to turn away and walk back to my house. There were a couple of ways back, but I decided to go back the way I came, back past the pavilion and playground. It was still cold and foggy. The pavilion came into sight, I walked towards it. There was no one sitting at the tables. I walked past a few people walking their dogs, each giving a friendly nod, and continued on their way.

I stood on the sidewalk in front of the pavilion. I decided to sit down at the table. I put my elbows on the table. I put my hands to my face and just covered my eyes. I did not know what I was feeling. I felt hurt, joy, sorrow, happiness, and dread all at once. Something that I did not want to feel again. I felt, deep down, that I really liked Derek. Especially after he kissed me, or I thought he kissed me. I did not know that Derek had that kind of confidence, but maybe he felt confident with me.

Why wouldn't his dad let me see him or just talk to him? I know he would have spoken to me. I had never heard Derek talk so much, but I guess I never really gave him a chance. I always walked right by him, went straight to my locker or classes. I always saw him walking the hallways being made fun of.

His books were being thrown across the hallway, pushed, shoved, and made to feel inferior. The memories just swarmed through my head. Playing over and over. There was no pause, no fast forward, no stop, or rewind. I felt like I was going crazy.

I stood up and started walking home. I looked back at the gazebo, hoping that Derek would show up, but he didn't. I walked down the sidewalk, stepping on the numerous damp leaves. I put my hood up because the wind was starting to pick up, again, along with a mist. The walk home seemed like it took forever. Finally, when I looked up from my feet, I saw my house.

CHAPTER 7
TRUTH HURTS

I stood at the end of the block, staring at my house and the other houses on the block. We lived on a cul-de-sac. People were beginning to return home for the evening hours, and while others were heading out for weekend plans. My dad's car was in the driveway.

I started to walk towards my house, and I immediately smelled the spiced pumpkin and apple cider from the front door. It was almost four o'clock, and I ran into my mom, cleaning things up around the house, and Jordan was in her usual spot on the couch.

"Hey Jenn, how are you feeling? Where did you go?" my mom asked.

"Just for a walk. Nothing extraordinary. I am going to head up to my room and just lay down. I am pretty tired all of a sudden." I answered back.

"Okay, well, just let me know if you need anything. I will be making dinner soon." My mom said.

"Okay, sounds great," I answered back, walking up the stairs to my room.

Once in my room, I threw myself on my bed. I felt like crying, but I didn't; I just laid there. I looked toward my desk and stared at the medication that was lying there. I forgot to take my medication. I knew skipping my medication was not good, and I had to get back on it as soon as possible. I ripped open the bag and took out the bottle.

"...*Clozapine. Jennifer Bailey... Prescribed by Dr. Flora. Take 1 pill with water, every 12 hours...*"

I took one of the pills and laid in bed. I stared at the ceiling. I thought about getting a head start on my homework, but it was Saturday, and I was not in the mood. I kept thinking about what Derek had said to me. I wanted to speak to him again. I did not want him to rush off like that. I let him kiss me. I did not know if that was a mistake. *Was I just caught up in the moment?*

Derek was somewhat attractive, but I think his strange awkwardness made him less attractive to people. What he said to me didn't make him any more appealing. If anything, it was the opposite. His words troubled me, made me anxious. Instead of letting his dad lead the conversation, I should have demanded that I see him! I don't know if that would have changed his mind. It seemed like his dad was the only one home. I have only seen his mom at back-to-school nights, but nowhere else.

I tried to get my mind off of Derek by watching

35

television. Of course, nothing of interest was on. So I surfed from channel to channel. I could hear my mom from the other side of the door calling to me. Dinner was ready, and I changed into sweat pants and a hoodie.

Coming down the hallway towards the stairs, I could smell spaghetti. Basil, oregano, and garlic. The fall candles, again, pumpkin spice and apple cider. At the bottom of the stairs, to the right, was the living room. The TV was on the news channel, like always.

I sat down at the dining table. Mom always had placemats that fit the season. Summer, she always had palm trees, coconuts, and the ocean. Spring, the placemats were filled with all kinds of flowers. Daffodils, tulips, and geraniums. Winter, it was snowmen. Those were her favorite. When it came time for Christmas, there were Santa Clause, snowmen, and snowflakes. However, it was fall, so there were leaves. She had arranged them like they were falling from a tree. There is also a gated fence and a bench. For a placemat, I thought, that was very artistic.

I envisioned myself in a picture. There was a path beyond the gates, filled with trees that had bright colored leaves in the photo. Sitting along the trail, covered with different colored leaves, was a park bench. I wondered where that path would lead me if I was on it. Would it be a never-ending walk? A chill in the air? Bright colored leaves falling from the trees, and crows cawing? Or, would the path lead me to a secluded house sitting on a hill? Lights were on, but never close enough to know what was going on inside.

Maybe a perfect moment with a family getting ready to sit down to dinner and enjoy each other's company? I would never know, but I could imagine what type of path it might be. These thoughts always came to me. What I would imagine as a perfect night at home, spending it with family or enjoying a regular night. I could look at a simple piece of art, such as a placemat or a drawing, and be able to put myself in its image. Living an endless number of realities.

Sitting down to dinner, I felt calmer and more relaxed. I felt like nothing else mattered as things were as they should be. I was having dinner with my family and enjoying their company. I talked to my mom, dad, and sister at the dinner table about how each other's day went. It was comforting.

The whole house felt comforting, exactly as Mom made it. The outside world was just that, the outside world. We had our place of serenity inside our home. Mom was still bringing out all of the fall decorations; the pumpkins and the towels with leaves falling from the trees. Which, to me, felt joyful.

"How did your day go? How was your doctor's appointment? Did it go okay?" My dad asked. My dad didn't really talk much. My father was a stern man, and he cared, very much, about his work.

"It was fine. I got a refill on my medications, and everything went okay." I answered back while putting down my fork.

"Did you do anything afterward? Did you go anywhere?" my father asked.

"I went for a walk, but nothing else really," I looked at him.

"The Kretins called. They said you showed up at their house and wanted to speak with Derek. They said you had just talked to him in the park and really wanted to speak with him. When they told you no, you looked confused and in disarray," my father said.

"The Kretins? Derek Kretin? No, Dad, I went for a walk and nothing else. I have had a lot on my mind." I said. It was the only response I could come up with, and it was the truth.

I looked at my father, confused, wondering what he was talking about. I tried to remember if I had even walked by the Kretin's house. I remember Derek as a very unpopular kid, and he was constantly made fun of at school. I did not want to be associated with him, primarily because of my already low social status at school.

"So you didn't go by there asking to speak to Derek?" Dad asked.

"No, not that I remember," I answered back.

My dad looked at my mom awkwardly, and he then smiled at me and said nothing more. My family was finishing dinner, and I took my plate to the sink to rinse it off. I helped clear more dishes from the table before heading back to my room.

38

"I am going to go upstairs; I am tired and just want to sleep," I said to both of my parents.

"Okay, that's fine, just try to get ahead on your homework you have missed a lot," they said back to me.

"Okay, I will," as I turned up the stairs.

Why were my mom and dad talking about Derek Kretin? He was the most unpopular and hated kid in the school. He always wore black, his hair was longer than average, and he was mischievous. That is not the type of guy I want to be associated with if I want to fit in. I laid down in bed and thought about my life and how I wanted it to go. I should probably get working on my homework, first of all, if I want to go anywhere in life.

Soon, my sister came into my room and just stared. Her look confused me...

"What is it? I am just laying here and thinking," I said to my sister as she was standing at the door.

"I am just wanting to know if you are okay. You have been acting strange lately, and I feel, as your sister, that I should talk about this with you," she explained, crossing her arms. Jordan sat on my bed, looking at me. It felt like she almost felt sorry for me, and I couldn't figure out why. I just stared at her back in dead silence.

"Are you okay with everything that happened at school? I worry about you. You don't even take notice about what happened or why it happened," my sister said, sitting on my bed.

I looked at her, still confused. Am I missing something? I had been to school every day, surprisingly. I honestly did not know what she was talking about. I just stared at her and let her talk.

"You know that Derek Kretin committed a mass shooting at your school, right?" Jordan asked, immediately standing up.

"What?!" I answered back in disbelief.

"He killed twenty-five people and injured at least thirty-five kids at YOUR school." She answered back.

I leaned back on my bed with my back against the wall. I looked at her in complete confusion. I was starting to get defensive. I had seen Derek walking through the hallways, going to class, and getting good grades. Now, she is telling me that he killed a bunch of people at my school! I think I would remember that! *Wait, is that why Lacy never texted me back…*

"What are you talking about? He didn't do that. I have seen him, and he is alive." I answered back.

"Do you remember what happened that day? There were so many kids killed all because of Derek Kretin, and it made National news. How could you not know about it? Everyone has been making remarks about Derek and how he was weird and a social outcast," Jordan answered, throwing her arms in the air.

I just sat there on my bed and couldn't believe

what I was hearing. She might have been using Derek as a scapegoat.

"Jordan, Derek is a good guy and wouldn't pull off something like a mass shooting. I get it he's socially awkward, but that doesn't mean he's a murderer." I said to her.

"He killed your friends or classmates in cold blood," as Jordan stood there looking down at me.

"What, friends? Plus, Derek is at home; I have been talking to him at the park for the past couple of afternoons. Derek is fine." I answered back in a raised voice.

My sister actually gave me a newspaper, and the headline read, "*Mass Shooting at King High School.*"

I couldn't believe what I was seeing, and I began to read the article. *"Gunman enters main hallway of school and opens fire. The Gunman killed a wide variety of students, 25 total. Law enforcement seeking motive states bullying as a possibility."*

"You believe that this was Derek Kretin? He brought in a rifle and two handguns to just kill a bunch of people at school? Do they know that it was Derek?" I asked Jordan. "The police officers were never able to get him into custody. So what? Is he just wandering the streets alone? Awaiting a manhunt which was almost impossible to do, seeing as Derek knew exactly where to go?"

"He committed murder, okay, Jennifer? He is not a good guy, no matter what you think he is."

41

"Unless proven guilty in the court of law, Jordan!" I shouted back at her.

"He won't be proven guilty in the court of law, Jennifer!" Jordan shouted back, turning away from me and putting her hands on her head. Jordan looked at me, and I could see that she was frustrated. She just shook her head at me, and I just stared back in anger. I tried to calm down and catch my breath.

"You don't get it, Jordan; I have been talking to Derek, okay? He wouldn't do something like that. Derek is at home, and I am telling you the truth," I tried to speak to her calmly.

"He's not at home, Jennifer! Okay? What can I do to make you see?" Jordan put her hands on her head and then covered her eyes, still shaking her head.

"Look, maybe you should just leave. You don't believe me, and I don't want to have this fight anymore," I told Jordan as I sat on my bed with tears in my eyes.

Jordan left my room. She looked back at me, tears of frustration in her eyes. I sat on my bed just staring at the door, wiping the tears from my eyes. I shook my head and laid down.

I looked up at the ceiling, thinking about everything Derek and I talked about. I really didn't know him at all. I reached for the newspaper that Jordan had handed me, and I still refused to believe it! I threw the newspaper aside. Derek did not seem innocent by any means, but I don't think he could do anything like that.

On the other hand, Derek was picked on every day by the kids at school. Did Derek even have any friends? I would never see him talk to anyone. Derek didn't belong to any clubs, cliques, or sports. It did not matter though, being a social outcast and committing mass murder were utterly different. I did not care what Jordan said. I talked to Derek for the past week, and he did not seem like that type of person.

I started to get ready for bed. I pulled the covers out of my bed and laid down. I turned on my side and laid there, wiping tears from my eyes. Eventually, I fell asleep.

"Why are you looking at me like that?" Derek asked.

"Did you shoot up the school?" I asked Derek directly, and Derek just looked at me and stared with his cold eyes. "I asked you a question, did you shoot up the school? Did you kill a bunch of our classmates?"

"I don't want to, but there's no other way." He said back to me.

"You 'don't want to?' As in you haven't done it?" I said back to Derek.

"They don't deserve to live, and they don't know what they are living for. People are bad, and fate doesn't take sides, Jennifer." Derek said back.

CHAPTER 8
ALONE

I woke up in a cold sweat. I did not know where I was. I finally realized I was in my room after looking around. I looked at my clock; it was 6 in the morning. Fifteen-minute before, I had to start getting ready for school. I looked at my ceiling, then to my closet, thinking about what to wear. I sat up in bed and looked at the calendar. Sunday, September 10th, 2002. After realizing it was Sunday, I laid back down in bed. I tried to go back to sleep but had no luck. I was already awake, and my dad gently knocked on the door as he cracked it open so he could speak to me.

"Hey Jenn, how did you sleep?" he asked from the doorway.

"Umm, fine, Dad. Yeah," I said, trying not to make eye contact.

"Okay, well, we're all downstairs if you need us," he gently shut the door. I could hear his head down the hallway towards the stairs.

I put on some clothes decided to go for another

walk. I do not know why I wanted to go for a walk; something told me to just go. I looked outside the window. It was nice. The sun was peeking in and out from behind the clouds as they passed. I threw on a short sleeve shirt and some jeans, no hoodie today. I brushed my hair, put it in a ponytail in front of my mirror, took my medication, and headed downstairs. I stopped midway down the stairs. Mom, Dad, and Jordan were eating breakfast at the dining table.

"Hey Jenny, do you want some breakfast?" Mom asked, setting her coffee mug down.

"Oh, no thanks, Mom. I think I am just going to go for a walk this morning." I continued to the front door. As I opened the door, I looked back at my family, and they were looking at me as I walked outdoor.

I began to walk down the driveway and towards the sidewalk. I did not know where I was going. Our house was at the bottom of a hill, and it took about fifteen minutes to reach the top of it. I continued into the next neighborhood. I was passed by families out enjoying their Sunday morning. As I walked through the next neighborhood, I came to the elementary school. I walked towards one of the three playgrounds that surrounded the school. The gravel crunching under my feet as I walked toward the swing set. The school was abandoned, abandoned on the weekend.

I decided to sit on one of the swings and kicked my feet, propelling myself back and forth. As I was swinging, I felt my phone vibrate. I quickly pulled it out of my pocket. It was Lacy! I quickly answered.

"Lacy! Hey! I haven't heard from you in forever!" I exclaimed. I started swinging faster in excitement.

"Hey! I know I have been so busy lately, but I just wanted to say 'hi.'" Lacy said back.

"I haven't even seen you at school. Have you been sick?" I asked, holding my head back.

"I have been at school, Jenn, just really busy with classes." She said.

"Oh, okay, I haven't seen you, and usually I do. I mean, at least walking down the hallways or something. I didn't want to text you, seeming like I was desperate or anything," I said, a little confused, trying to keep the awkward silence to a minimum.

Lacy said nothing to me. I just held my phone and looked around, and I pulled the phone away to see if I had lost service.

"Lacy? Are you there?" I asked.

"Yeah, I'm here. How are you feeling, Jenn? What did your doctor say?" Lacy asked.

"What? Nothing, Lacy, the same as usual." I said, annoyed.

"Okay, but, Jenn, I just wanted to make sure you are taking your medication. You have been really off lately, and I am worried about you." Lacy said to me.

I kept swinging on the swing. I started to see a pattern of people asking me if I was okay. My doctor, sister, parents, and now Lacy and I did not know their deal.

"Yes, Lacy, I am taking my medication. I was off it for about four or five days because I ran out, but I got a refill. I'm fine," I said to Lacy reassuringly.

"Okay, well, I got to go, Jenn. I have to do homework. I will see you at school tomorrow. Try and get some homework done yourself, okay?" Lacy said.

"Okay, I will, Lacy. I'm glad you called."

I hung up.

I was starting to get worried. Everyone kept asking how I was feeling and if I was taking my medication. I knew I had been, except for the few days that I was out. I was confused and a little bit angry. I felt like I was about to cry. Everyone was treating me like I was sick, but I am not ill. I am fine. I feel fine. I looked back at my phone and stood up from the swing.

I started walking to other playgrounds near the elementary school. I walked through the grass. It was damp from the rain or maybe the sprinklers. The other playground had a gazebo and a swing set that was smaller than the other one. I sat down at the table under the pavilion. I sat there wondering why I was even there. I looked around at all the houses that surrounded the school and the pavilion. Everything looked calm and quiet. There were not many people out. I sat there for another thirty minutes before I decided to head home.

As I was standing up, a couple was walking by from a nearby house. It was Derek Kretins' parents. *Dad just asked me about Derek the other night, right?* I decided to pull out my phone and pretend I was texting someone. As they got closer, I could hear their conversation.

"What do you want me to do?" Derek's dad asked his mom.

"We need to do something." She said.

"He is acting so strange, and he is so withdrawn. He won't talk to us or anyone, for that matter." Derek's dad said as he continued to walk the path.

"I think we need to get him some help, whether you think I am right or not." His mom said, looking at Derek's dad.

"Well, he won't talk to us. What makes you think he is going to sit and talk with a psychiatrist?" He said.

The conversation started to fade as they walked further away from the pavilion. I put my phone down and thought to myself, *obviously, there was something wrong with Derek.* I think I knew what was wrong with Derek. He was socially awkward and did not have many friends, but there were plenty of antisocial and awkward kids, which should not cause parents to worry. It really sparked my interest because Dad was talking about Derek yesterday.

I put my phone away and started walking down the same path as Derek's parents. They were still in my line of sight, but I was far behind them. They turned down a different way and started walking in that direction, and I stopped and stared at them until I lost sight.

I turned down the path to my house. The walk home felt like an eternity. Thoughts were starting to get jumbled in my mind again. *When was the last time I had heard from Lacy? Why did that gazebo feel so familiar? How long have I been walking? Haven't I passed that house already?* I was trying to gather my thoughts, *look at the leaves on the ground* when I looked up and realized I had made it home.

Was I standing right in front of my house? I walked in. I looked at my phone, it was already one o'clock. I did not realize I spent that much time at the park. I saw my parents sitting at the table talking. Jordan was not there, though, which means she probably went out with her never-ending circle of friends. I said my usual "hi" to my parents and headed to my room. As I walked up the stairs, I wanted to call Lacy again. As soon as I got to my room, I pulled out my phone and dialed her number.

The phone rang until her voicemail was answered. I hung up tried again, but it was the same, voicemail. Eventually, I just sat down on my bed and then laid down. I looked at the medication sitting on the desk. I turned my head away from it. I thought about how everyone was so intent on taking this medication, but it was my choice! I could take it when I wanted. I sighed heavily. Laid in bed and lost myself to my thoughts.

CHAPTER 9
IN TOO DEEP

I woke up startled. I sat up in bed and looked around. I realized it was morning, six o'clock. The calendar read "Tuesday." *Wait, I thought it was Monday?* I realized I was going to be late for school. I rushed around my room. What had happened to Monday? I could not remember eating dinner on Sunday. I could not even remember Monday at all. I tried to get ready as fast as I could. I started brushing my hair. I looked at the calendar again. Tuesday, September 12th, 2002.

Suddenly, something inside of me switched and told me to relax, get ready for school. It will be just another day at school. All I had to do was get through today and the next four days. Then it would be the weekend. I finished getting dressed. I wanted to walk by the pavilion; I was in a hurry to get there. Derek would be there so I could talk to him. Nobody understood him. Maybe that was the problem.

Everyone was set on the fact that he was the monster, but I knew differently. Derek would be at the playground, and we would talk about what other people were saying about him. He probably felt angry and alone, exactly how I would think if people said the same about me.

I started along the sidewalk and through the neighborhoods. People were hustling around in their houses. Cars were starting in the driveway. Families were sitting at their tables drinking coffee, smiling, and talking. I thought about how nice their lives must be as I walked past their houses. *Why couldn't mine be nice? I had a family. Why couldn't I wake up to breakfast and everyone drinking coffee, talking, and smiling together?* I was jealous. My family was not like that as Mom would greet me in the morning. She would speak to me during dinner, but that was it. I did not have a friendly family to talk to in the early morning. No meaningful conversations during dinner.

I continued walking down the sidewalk, past the elementary school. There is the pavilion. I walked toward it, but no one was there. The sun was shining, but it was not warm. It sure beats the rain and fog, though. I reached the pavilion, but Derek was not there. I looked toward the two swings on the playground. They swayed gently in the wind. I sat at one of four tables under the gazebo and waited for Derek to arrive. I waited for 45 minutes. Still, no sign of him. *Was Derek avoiding me? Did he have any interest in talking to me after I went to his house and demanded to speak with him?*

After an hour of waiting, it was apparent that Derek was not coming. I reluctantly headed to school. The school was the last place I wanted to be, but I had no choice. I did not care about my grades or attendance. I wanted to see Derek. I had so many questions that only he could answer. I looked back at the swing as I walked towards the school. *Where are you, Derek?*

This walk seemed longer than any other walk. I eventually reached the school, and I heard echoes of non-stop chatter from everyone outside. The echoes turned to a dull roar as I entered the hallways. I headed straight for my locker and grabbed my books for math class. I should have known that math was not the class to have right in the morning, but that's what I get for making a poor decision.

I made my way towards Room 120 for math class. Ben Fuller caught up with me in the hall and tried to make small talk. Ben was an average kid, medium height, blonde hair, and wore average clothes. Nothing too trendy, fashionable enough to be ignored entirely. Ben was not popular by any means. Like many other kids, he was subject to the non-stop bullying this school had to offer.

"Hey Jenn, how are you doing? Is everything okay?" Ben asked as we continued to walk down the hallway together.

"Umm yeah, things are fine, nothing really new," I replied.

"Okay, I was just making sure. This school can be overbearing, especially nowadays." Ben said back to me.

"Why do you say that? Are there some mysterious

and horrific events that have manifested at this school over the last few days?" I scoffed.

Ben looked at me, puzzled and without a response. He only stared. *Great, another staring contest…*

"Okay, Jenn, I'm not trying to be blunt, or offensive, or anything, but this school did *just* have a mass shooting and a lot of people that were killed and injured," Ben said. He was trying to hide his frustration.

"Derek Kretin, right? He committed some mass murder at this school, right? Well, I have seen Derek, and he's at home. Which is exactly where he should be. Considering that everyone is accusing him of all these terrible things." I said, raising my voice.

"Jennifer, Derek is not at home. I don't know who you talked to," Ben started to say before I interrupted him.

"Derek! I talked to Derek! I even talked to his father at his house!" I was yelling now.

"Okay, did you see him at home?" Ben asked, trying to get me to lower my voice.

"Well… no. I didn't see him at his house, but his Dad told me he didn't want to talk about Derek. He didn't let me see him at the house. Although, I did see and talk to Derek in the park next to the elementary school not too far from here. I did see him. We talked at least a couple of times these past few days." I said back to Ben.

Ben stared at me with confusion on his face. Like he could not believe what I was saying.

"Okay, forget it, I have to get to class before I am late. You should probably do the same," I said to Ben.

Math class was a blur. I could not pay attention. The only thing I could think about was Derek. *Why hadn't I seen him in the park today?* The teacher's voice echoed in the background, and I did not understand what she was teaching or how to solve the problems that she was putting on the overhead screen.

The bell rang, and everyone got up from their seats. There was a rush for the door. My following classes all went by reasonably fast. Social studies, language arts, and science. All much easier than math. It is usually easier to engage in those classes, but again my mind wandered. *Just let this day be over with!*

The final bell rang. I rushed to my locker, put all the books I did not need in it, and shut it. I threw my backpack over my shoulders and headed out the door. I could hear two girls talking about Derek. Dianna and Casey. Both are typical cheerleaders. Beautiful, blonde, and full of gossip. I could hear some of their conversations as I walked past them.

"I just miss them, you know?" Casey said.

"I know, but there's nothing we can do about it. It's done." Dianna said back to Casey as she started to cry.

The two hugged, and Dianna started crying. A few more people came towards them, and it became an actual group hug. I stood there and stared, and not knowing what to think.

"Excuse me, Jennifer. Do you have a problem? Why don't you just run along with home instead of sitting here, staring at us, and creeping us out?" Dianna said to me as I finally turned and made my way to the parking lot and onto the sidewalk that led home.

I tried to fight back the tears as I walked home. Why do people treat me like that? I saw that people were sad, but no one asked if I was miserable. Nobody seemed to care, at least not at school. I wiped away my tears and continued home.

57

CHAPTER 10
FAR FROM ALONE

I strolled down the sidewalk and wondered why guys and other girls liked to be around gossip. The only thing those girls knew how to do was put people down. If you weren't in their clique, life was rough. I did not know how I would ever be accepted. All the popular kids treated me like I was invisible.

I watched my feet as I walked down the sidewalk. I looked up to see the playground and pavilion, and I was still too far away to see if anyone was sitting there. As I got closer to the pavilion, I noticed Derek was not there. I looked around for him, but he never showed up. I dropped to the sidewalk. I watched the gazebo as if it were going to move.

It was starting to get cloudy. I must have been sitting on that sidewalk for an hour. A jogger and his dog startled me. I quickly got up off the sidewalk and walked towards one of the tables under the gazebo. The jogger looked at me with concern, and I waved at him to let him know that I was alright. He waved back, then continued on his way.

I started towards the sidewalk and began the walk back home. I looked back to see the swings swaying in the wind, internally frustrated at my expectation of Derek being there today. The wind was growing intense, and it was getting colder. I could see my house in the distance. Realizing how I was almost there, I quickened my pace.

I arrived at the front door. Mom had started pulling out more fall decorations. She had all of the decorations placed strategically on the porch. There was a Welcome mat with different colored leaves on it. More reminders of why I love this time of year.

"Hey honey, how was school? Did everything go okay?" Mom asked as I entered the door.

"Yeah, everything was fine, and it was just regular school," I sighed.

"Okay, well, I am making dinner, and it should be ready pretty soon." She said.

"Okay, Mom, but I might just actually lay down. I am not feeling very well and think I just need to rest for tonight." I said.

"Okay, well, I will save you a plate for later if you get hungry," she said to me as I headed to my room.

"Thanks, Mom," I answered, without turning back to her.

I tossed my backpack on the floor, threw on some sweats and a hoodie, and sat on the bed. I stared at the floor in a state of confusion. I felt numb. Tears started

59

to well up in my eyes. I laid down on my side and slowly drifted off to sleep.

I was jerked out of sleep. I looked around to see it was still dark out. It was midnight. *Not late for school*. I took a deep breath and fell back asleep, startled awake by my alarm clock. It was set for six-thirty. I threw myself out of bed and changed quickly. I was going to be late if I did not pick up the pace.

"Hey Mom, I have to go. I slept in really late, and I am going to be really late. Sorry, I can't talk about it right now, but I will talk to you later," as I shouted through the house.

"Okay, I'll see you after school." She answered back, neither one of us making eye contact that morning.

I darted out the door and started walking to school. I honestly did not want to walk by the gazebo today, but it was the shortest route to school. My fast walk turned into a jog down the sidewalk, past the elementary school, and then by the gazebo. I looked at the table to see Derek there. Just sitting at the table and looking down at the ground. Derek's hair was covering his face. He had on his black jacket, blue jeans, and black gloves. I stood there staring at him. He did not notice I was standing there yet.

"Jennifer, talk to him. Talk to him. Talk to him. Talk to him." Said an Unknown Male voice.

"Jennifer, you're just standing there. Jennifer, your standing." Said Another Unknown Male voice.

I shook my head and covered my eyes. I wanted to cry, but this was not the time or place. Derek is there. I see him, and I know he is there; there is no doubt about it.

"Talk to him and die. Talk to him and die. You will die. Sooner or later, you will have no luck. Die," A Sinister Male voice growled.

"No. No. No. No. No!" I muttered, still shaking my head.

I uncovered my eyes with tears are streaming down my cheeks. Derek was looking in my direction now, staring at me, a competition of glares that was growing old. I walked toward him and sat at the table across from Derek. Derek said nothing. I thought to myself, *maybe he could ask how I was doing. Why was I crying?* Instead, Derek just sat there looking at me with his unkind eyes.

"Why do I always find you here? Why is it always at this park and nowhere else? What are you doing? Are you on the run because you decided to kill a bunch of our fellow classmates in one of the most horrific murders anyone has ever seen?" I asked intently and slamming my hand on the table.

"I told you that you wouldn't be able to change anything. I told you what I was intending to do, and you obviously weren't listening," Derek replied, staring just as intently as I was at him.

"Jennifer is sitting down," Another Unknown Male voice said.

I looked around; no one else was there. Only Derek and I.

"Why did you kill all of those people, Derek?" I asked, looking directly at him.

"What, do you actually feel sorry for the people that I killed? Because if I am not mistaken, those people tortured you in the exact same way they did me. Don't give me any of this sympathy bullshit Jennifer." There was darkness in his voice.

Derek stopped talking, then looked up at me. It was a sinister look as if he wanted to kill me. His hair was covering his eyes. There was a weird smile on his face. I started to feel uneasy about even being around him.

"Are you afraid of me? You should be! Everyone should be! I am done being pushed aside and constantly ridiculed every day! People need to know and remember that people are not who they say they are. Like me, you would never know how evil I really was because I hid it from everyone.

Now, I am the one that everyone needs to fear, and that's one of the things that I longed for in this life, and now I got it. I got people's attention now, and they will never question again who I was because I left my mark and secured my spot in history. People will want to forget, but they will realize they can't because what I did is so horrific that people will never forget because it's engraved in their minds. They will remember me; they will remember my name and not the names of the people I killed," Derek said, with evil in his eyes.

"Jennifer, you will die. You are nobody, and nobody will miss you," said Another Unknown Male.

I tried to hold my ground. It was getting difficult to hold back my tears. There was so much going on, I could barely handle it. There were too many people talking to me all at once, and I could not sort it out.

"Derek, I went to your house. I followed you to your house right after you kissed me. Which I really couldn't feel, by the way. I knocked on your door and asked your dad if I could see you. He pretended like you weren't even there and got so angry with me that he slammed the door in my face. Why would he do something like that?" I asked Derek, even more frustrated.

"I wasn't at my house, Jennifer," Derek said back to me.

"Yes, you were. I saw you walk to your house, and I followed you," I said back angrily.

"Right. Okay, did you see me go into my house, or did you just see me walk in that general direction?" Derek asked.

"I guess you were walking in that general direction. I don't know, and I just know that you were headed to your house that you have lived in for quite some time now." I answered and stood up from the table. Derek continued to sit down and started to look up at me.

63

"Jennifer is standing up now," Another Unknown Male came across.

"Well, yeah, of course, I am standing up. I am angry and extremely frustrated by this entire conversation." I answered back.

Derek sat there staring up at me with his evil smirk. I tried to look at something else. I could see a family walking their dog approaching Derek and me. They looked like a happy family just taking a walk. As they crossed my path, the whole family smiled at me and waved. I gave a half-smile and waved back.

The family did not seem to notice Derek. As the family walked by, I looked at Derek. He continued to look up at me with arrogance. Derek then proceeded to fold his hands together with his black gloves still on. He then began to scoff and shake his head. I glared at him with frustration.

"Are you satisfied, Jenn? Do you finally see now?" Derek asked as he continued to look up at me.

"Satisfied with what? What are you talking about? Why does everything have to be a god damn mystery with you? No, seriously, I want to know" I demanded.

"Jennifer. You're mad. You're angry. It's bad. Die!" An Unknown Male voice came across.

"Kill yourself, Jennifer; this will all be over with. Just kill yourself," An Unknown Female voice came across.

"No, I don't want to kill myself!" I screamed.

He started to smile with his usual creepy smile. I looked back at him, tilted my head, and rolled my eyes. I turned my head back towards Derek, and I tried to make sense of what was happening.

"I killed myself," Derek said.

"What? Who was that? Was that you, Derek, or someone else?" I asked.

"I am the only one here, I think," Derek said back.

"What do you mean you killed yourself? You're here, you're talking to me, and I can touch your hand," I said as I reached for his hand.

This time, Derek didn't pull away but let his hand stay on the table with mine over his. I quickly pulled away and put my hand over my mouth. His hand was ice cold, and I could barely feel anything. He took one of my hands, then placed his other hand on top. I could not handle him; all I could feel was cold. I thought, maybe this is what death felt like. As he had my hands in his, I looked at him and finally just fell to a seated position on the table. Tears were welling up in my eyes.

"Why did you kill yourself? Why would you do that? Is your life really that bad that you needed to leave this world? How am I talking to you if your, if you're dead." I asked with my voice starting to shake.

"I don't know how you're talking to me, Jenn. I just end up showing up when you're thinking about me." Derek said.

"No, no, that is not true. I have been thinking about you all the time and yesterday you were not here. You were not at this playground or table. You were gone, and I waited for you; you never showed up. So don't tell me that you only show up when I think about you because that is absolute bullshit!" I yelled at Derek.

Derek then stood up. He let go of my hand, then stood right in front of me, very close to my face. The wind was picking up again, and I did not know if it was getting colder or Derek standing so close to me.

"Okay, you're going to have to give me a little bit more than you killed yourself," I said to Derek as he kept standing incredibly close to my face.

"I told you, I killed who I needed to kill, and I wasn't going to go to jail, so I just killed myself," Derek said.

"With your own gun? The same guns you used to kill our fellow classmates at our school?" I shouted and cried at the same time. I then started to shake and couldn't believe that I was having this conversation.

"Death is a way out. You can try it. Just die, Jennifer," An Unknown Male told me.

I shook my head and began to cry even more. I started to collapse. Derek then came over, trying to catch me. He brought me slowly to the ground under the pavilion. I could not get over how ice-cold he was. I pulled away from him and started bawling. I put my head on my knees. I was expecting Derek to leave, but

66

instead, he stayed.

Derek ended up sitting on the ground next to me, but now he wasn't touching me. Derek was just looking at me, but instead of the creepy grin, he actually looked a little bit sad yet annoyed at the same time. I could not understand how I was talking to Derek if he was, in fact, dead. The dead don't come back and talk to people. That is just not the way it is. It does not work that way.

Derek then started to lean towards me as if he wanted to kiss me again. I put my hand on his chest and looked at him. I did not know what to think. I liked Derek, but how could I kiss a guy that just committed one of the worse school shootings. Derek then grabbed my hand and kissed me anyway. I believe I was starting to kiss him back, but it felt bizarre. It was ice cold, it did not feel right, but a part of me really enjoyed it. I did find Derek somewhat attractive regardless of his social status. Derek and I have become extremely close after the conversations that we had.

The kiss was becoming very passionate. Then it hit me again, this person was dead. *How am I kissing this person?* It did not feel like I was kissing a person. It felt as if I were getting closer to death. When I pulled away from him, life felt like it was coming back to me. He continued to lean his head towards mine. I put my hand on his face and looked at him. I had no words. He stared at me, waiting for me to speak. I looked at his eyes from a completely different perspective now. I looked at him, but this time it was a look of sorrow.

"Derek, your dead. You're not supposed to be in this world anymore, and you chose to leave," as I kept my hand on his face.

"You are the only person that I have been able to connect with, let alone talk to or kiss," Derek said.

"Look, I just know that you're not supposed to be here, and I can't do this. I have really grown to like you, and I think I have got to know you, but this can't happen between us, Derek." I said to him as I finally pulled my hand away.

"Why can you see me and talk to me, Jenn? How do you know you're not dead? I have sat at this table under this gazebo for quite some time now, and no one has ever noticed me except you. You know as well as I do how many people walk this path, and I am invisible to everyone, apart from you. You could be dead and not know it." Derek frustratingly said to me while pointing his finger at me.

"I am not dead, Derek. I am not dead." I firmly said as I stood up from the table.

"I could have killed you, Jenn. The shooting? Starting to come together for you. Is anything ringing a bell?" Derek said and then started to smile at me and stare at me with his yet again creepy smile. His smile then faded; it turned into a stare. Derek turned away he started towards the table at the gazebo. Derek sat down, put his arms and hands on the table spread out.

"Just kill yourself, Jennifer. This could all be over with once you kill yourself," The Unknown Male said to me.

I stood on the sidewalk, still facing Derek. All of a sudden, it hit me. This guy was telling me to kill myself, and it will all be over with. Right then and there, I knew I was alive, and Derek was lying. I was not dead, and I was not finished yet. I stood there fully confident, and I finally stopped crying.

"I am not dead Derek, you didn't kill me for whatever reason that may be," I said to him.

"You don't know that. You still don't have an answer as to how you're talking to me and seeing me." Derek said back.

"I do know that actually because he just told me to kill myself and get it over with. With that, I know that I am alive," I said to Derek confidently and talked at a swift pace.

"Who told you that?" Derek asked.

"This guy that I know, I don't think you know him," I told Derek, starting to look away from him.

"When did this shooting take place? What day?" as I raised my voice to Derek.

"September 1st. Almost a while ago now." Derek said to me.

"It's September 13th Derek, this didn't happen a while ago. It literally happened thirteen days ago." I explained to him.

Suppose this school shooting happened on September 1st, and all these kids were either killed or seriously injured. Why is everyone still in school? Wouldn't school be shut down? The amount of blood and gore would alone cause the school to shut down, but I have been going to school, attending classes like normal. However, kids keep talking about the shooting and how tragic it was to lose so many people. The newspaper even had the front page of the massacre at King High School.

"Did it happen September 1st of this year or last year?" I asked Derek.

"It was a long time ago, Jenn," Derek answered back.

If it indeed happened a long time ago, as Derek had claimed, then why are people acting and talking about it like it was a current event?

"Jennifer, you're going to die anyway. Just get it over with and kill yourself. You have nothing to live for anymore." The Female voice spoke. I tried to ignore the voice and looked at Derek, concerned, yet I was frightened.

"Okay, I have to go, Derek. It is about 5 o'clock, and my mom will worry me if I don't come home soon. I have been out here talking to you for three hours, and which is surprisingly the longest conversation I have ever had with you." I told Derek.

"I will see you soon, Jennifer. You know where I will always be. I'll be waiting for you," Derek said as

I walked away from the pavilion. I looked back. To my surprise, Derek was still there, and he was still looking at me. As soon I was out of his sight, I ran home as fast as I could.

CHAPTER 11
STAY OR RUN

I felt like I had been running forever when I started to see my house. I stopped running to catch my breath. I fell into someone's lawn, sat there, and began to cry. I couldn't believe what had just happened. Questions kept running through my mind. *Should I have stayed there at the playground and talked with Derek? Should I have asked more questions? Why was he so short with me? He told me that he was dead. Derek told me he killed himself during the massacre. Was I talking to a dead person?*

I sat there crying harder. I turned around to see the owner of the house peering out of his window at me. I quickly stood up, brushed myself off, and started towards my house. I tried to compose myself before getting home. I did not want Mom to notice. However, she would see that I was late, she would ask where I was for the last three hours. I tried to come up with an excuse before I made it to the front door.

I noticed that my mom had done more decorating for the fall. There were pumpkins and scarecrows on the porch now, greeting me as I walked into the house, along with the smell of pumpkin spice candles and dinner cooking.

"Jenn, where have you been? It's 5:30, and I thought you were going to be home a lot earlier." Mom said. "Is everything okay?"

"Yeah, everything is fine. I am just going to head upstairs for a little bit," I said back to her.

"Okay, well, I am a little late on dinner, and it probably won't be ready till about seven. I wanted to get more fall decorations up," Mom said, smiling.

"Okay, Mom, that sounds good. Just let me know when everything is ready, and I'll be down," I said back to her, walking up the stairs.

I was in my room, and I took off my backpack and threw it on the floor. Instead of sitting on my bed, I collapsed to the floor. I was in disarray about what had happened today. I looked up at my desk to see my prescription. I sat there, sighed, and realized that I didn't take my medication today. I immediately went to grab it, took double the dose with some water from the nightstand. I figured I would take two since I had missed a dose.

"Why are you crying, Jennifer? Did you realize you were supposed to die?" said the female voice.

I shook it off, continued to sit on my floor, and stared at my wall.

"She's going to start crying again." Said The Unknown Male voice.

As a matter of fact, I did start crying. I could not help it, but I felt the need to with everything that had happened today. I covered my eyes with my hand and continued to cry. All of a sudden, there was a knock at the door. Mom was standing in the doorway.

"Honey, what's wrong? Is everything okay? Why are you crying?" She asked me.

"It's nothing, Mom. Really," I answered back, wiping away my tears.

She continued to look at me, clearly not convinced that things were okay.

"It's just these girls that were giving me a hard time; I don't know, it just hasn't been a good day. I'm glad to be home, Mom. I just want to be home." I told her.

"Well, you are home. If you need to talk about anything, just let me know. I am always here, and you can talk to me about anything." She said.

"I know, thanks, Mom. I love you." I told her.

"I love you too, honey. I'll let you know when dinner is ready. Why don't you get started on some of your homework?" she suggested.

"Yeah, I will, Mom," nodding my head at the same time.

She closed my bedroom door. I could hear her footsteps receding down the hall, then down the stairs. The next thing I had to worry about was Jordan walking into my room. I really did not want to explain to her what was going on. She would not understand any of it anyway. If I told anyone that I was talking to Derek Kretin, everyone would think I was crazy. *Derek told me he was dead, that he killed himself. Yet, I was able to talk to him? Dead or alive, I know exactly who I had been talking to for the last week.* I know in my mind that it was real. I could not make something like this up, even if I wanted to. I went to bed and laid down.

Not more than ten minutes went by – or so I thought - when I heard my mom calling that it was time for dinner. I looked at my clock, 7:15, and it had been almost two hours! I quickly changed into some comfortable clothes and headed downstairs, and sat at the table. My dad and Jordan were home, and mom had made steak, mash potatoes, and salad.

"How are you feeling?" Dad asked, concerned.

"I'm fine, Dad. Really I am fine. Why does everyone keep asking about how I am feeling?" I said, looking at everyone at the table.

"Well, with the shooting, we all just wanted to make sure you were doing okay. Jordan had said she tried to talk to you about it, but you just kept defending Derek," he replied.

"Again, you do realize he killed and injured a bunch of your classmates?" Jordan snapped.

I looked at Jordan, shook my head, and glared. I looked back at Dad and Mom. They were at least giving me looks of sympathy rather than my sister coming at me full speed with inaccurate accusations. I stayed silent. MY FAMILY DIDN'T NEED TO KNOW whether I had talked to Derek in the last week or not because they obviously didn't understand.

"Can we just talk about something else?" I asked my whole family putting down my fork. They all looked at each other reluctantly, and silence fell over the table.

"Okay, now it's just too quiet. Let's talk about something, but just not about Derek or the shooting." I said to my family, looking at them with desperation.

"Jordan, how is school going?" Dad asked with a mouth full of salad.

"It's so great. Classes are going great, and there is going to be a get-together on Friday, but don't worry, Dad, all my homework will be done." Jordan said, sitting up straight in her chair.

I looked at both Mom and Dad as they smiled at Jordan.

"Good for you honey, I am glad things are going well, and we are both proud of the grades that you are getting," Mom said after taking a drink of water.

"Thank you," Jordan said as she took a bite of her salad.

I watched as everyone carried on their conversation without me. I stood up from the table, took my plate to the sink, and put it in the dishwasher.

76

I walked out of the kitchen and headed upstairs. Nobody said anything to me; they just let me go. I looked back when I was in the middle of the staircase, my family continuing their conversation.

I walked down the hallway to my room. I thought that I should probably get started on my homework, and I was getting behind in classes. As I walked into my room, I looked toward my closet to see Derek standing there.

CHAPTER 12
SURPRISE VISITOR

I shrieked and immediately closed my bedroom door. I stood there shocked before I could say anything.

"Jesus! What the hell are you doing here in my bedroom Derek?" I whispered loudly, holding my chest. I thought I was about to have a heart attack. "I wanted to see you, and you were thinking about me," Derek said, still standing by my closet. Derek was still wearing his black jacket, jeans, and gloves. His long straight hair was still covering part of his face as he was talking to me.

"What makes you think you can just come into my room like this?" I asked, still holding my chest. "Well, I'm here. What does it matter?" Derek said as he sat down on my desk chair.

"Did you come through the front door?" I whispered.

"Jenn, I told you already, I am dead. It doesn't matter how I got here. I came here to see you, and you are literally the only one I can talk to!" Derek said.

"You can talk to people Derek, you just choose not to, as I said before," I replied, standing in front of him now.

"Really? Okay, Jenn, what are these pills for? What do you take them for? I know you don't have a cold or the flu," he said, holding the pills in front of me.

I just stood there. Tears started to flood my eyes. I did not know what was happening.

"You're sick, Jenn. You don't belong in this world, and you might as well just die," The Female voice came again.

I shook my head and covered my eyes. I wiped the tears away, just staring at Derek. He looked at me without sympathy, only staring and giving me a creepy smile.

"These pills are for mental illness. Believe me, I know. My parents have taken me to numerous psychologists and psychiatrists, but these pills are different. They are not for anxiety or depression, and they are antipsychotics, Jennifer!" Derek yelled and stood up from the desk chair.

I started to back up and fell onto the bed. I looked up at him with tears in my eyes, not knowing what to say to him.

79

"So what are you trying to say, Derek? That I am psychotic? I am a lunatic?" I answered, sobbing, wiping the tears away as fast as I could.

"You can see me, and I'm dead, Jennifer. What else would you call it? What are you diagnosed with? The doctor must have given you a diagnosis, right?" Derek said, still standing over me.

"I don't know, okay! Look in my drawer; all of the paperwork from my doctors is in my desk!" I raised my voice, now standing eye to eye with him. Derek turned away. He went to my desk and opened the drawer. He found the folder with the paperwork. He began reading it, shuffling through papers. I wanted to stop him, but instead, I sat on the bed, knees tucked towards my chest.

Derek pulled out a piece of writing he began reading it very closely. He looked up at me. Again, no remorse, just hostility. I stopped crying. I started to feel scared. I did not know what to expect at that moment. I sat there waiting for Derek to say something for what seemed like forever.

CHAPTER 13
TRUTH IS IN THE EYE OF THE BEHOLDER

Derek stood there holding the paper in his hands, not saying anything. He looked and smirked at me.

"You're a psycho, Jennifer. You have been and always will be," The Male voice said.

"See, I told you. I knew you thought I was a psycho. So why are you in my bedroom? Why did you kiss me? Twice! If you know I am sick, why are you still here? Why would you want to be associated with a girl like me?" I raised my voice to Derek and stood up from my bed.

"I didn't say anything," Derek scoffed.

I looked at Derek, confused and angry. *Derek just said I was a psycho.*

"This paper says you were diagnosed with schizophrenia, Jennifer! For example, the voice you just answered to was not me." Derek said, shaking his head.

I ripped the paper away from his hands. Instead of Derek backing up after I made such a hostile movement towards him, he held his ground. My eyes were still filled with tears. *Is this why everyone was asking if I was taking my medication and asking if I was okay?* I backed away from Derek, turned around, and put my hands on my head. I looked back to see that he was still there, glaring at me. He looked as if he wanted to harm me.

"He's going to kill you. He wants to kill you, and he doesn't love you." The Female voice said.

"Did you kill all those people at our school, Derek?" I asked, wiping my tears.

"Yes, Jennifer! How many times do I have to tell you? I killed everyone that I wanted to kill, and I accomplished my mission in life. I am going to kill you, too," he said as he looked directly into my eyes.

"Did you kill Lacy? My best friend? My only friend?" I asked, standing at a close distance to Derek, completely disregarding the fact that he said he wanted to kill me.

"Yes, Jennifer. I killed Lacy, and I am not sorry

about it," Derek scoffed. He turned away from me once again, then looked directly at me, still very close to my face. Derek started to reach for my hand, but I immediately pulled away.

"You're the one saying I am *psychotic*, Derek? Do you even hear yourself or what you're saying to me? You said you killed my best friend, you want to kill me, and then want you to reach for my hand?" I stood back and tried to get away from him. Derek just looked at me, then sat back down in my desk chair. "What is wrong with you? How could you be so heartless and cold? You're the one that is psychotic, Derek!" I raised my voice, standing over Derek.

"I told you, I don't fit in this world. I think differently than other people. But just think about this for a second, Jennifer. Who is to say that I am psychotic because I want to kill people? What if our society was different? Society deems me psychotic because killing people is wrong, but what if it were the other way around? Then I would be completely normal, right? Then killing people wouldn't be wrong. Again, that's why I am saying I am not fit for this world and never will be. I think differently, and I can't help that," Derek continued to explain, looking at me keenly.

His words made me think. *I could see where he was coming from, but it still was not right. Derek could not just go around killing innocent people because he feels he needs or has the right to. He was wronged. He thought of my many reasons to sell*

himself the justice of following through with the act.
Killing people in "the ultimate" massacre is what he
saw as justice.

I heard a knock on my bedroom door. It startled
me enough to make me jump. I quickly turned toward
the door and then back to the desk chair. *Was Derek
gone?* I heard the knock again.

"Yes! What?" I yelled at the closed door, taking
hold of my hair and throwing it back. I was quickly
trying to catch my breath. As soon as I was at my
door, Jordan walked in. I looked at her, tilting my
head to suggest that she had interrupted me.

"Who are you talking to?" she asked, still holding
the doorknob.

"What? Nobody, Jordan, I was just reading an
assignment for school," I answered as I tried to look
for a textbook.

"For what class? I don't even see any of your
books out, Jenn." She said back to me, crossing her
arms.

I glared at her. It was none of her business what I
was doing in my own room anyway. *Everyone just
needed to back off and leave me alone for once!* I
tried to stop glaring and give her a more welcoming
look, but it just came off as awkward and disoriented.

"Yeah, well, I have a big test in world history, and it just helps to talk about the subject to myself, and I can remember it better," I said quickly, still playing with my hair. She was not convinced.

I could not help but notice that Jordan still looked terrific. *It is 8 o'clock on a school night. Who are you trying to impress?* I shook my head at her and rolled my eyes. Jordan did her best to smile at me but still had a look of concern. She shut the door and left without saying anything more.

Once the door was closed, I felt my knees buckle. I was breathing heavily. I did not know how she did not see Derek there, but I was thankful that she hadn't. I sat up on the floor against my bed, trying to gather myself. I could hear a conversation taking place downstairs in the kitchen between my parents. I opened my door ever so slightly, trying not to make a sound.

I stayed close to the ground. In our house, there was a balcony that lined the hallway. It had wooden posts and railing that you could see through to the ground level. I crawled down the hallway to get a better view. Jordan was seated on the last two steps. I looked past her to see both of my parents staring at her as if they wanted an answer. I had no idea what was going on, but I was going to find out.

CHAPTER 14
NO SECRETS

"Well, what did she say, Jordan?" Dad asked, sitting in the dining room chair that was facing the stairs.

"She was talking to someone, Dad, but I don't know who," Jordan said, leaning against the third stair.

"She's having hallucinations again, Dianna. She is talking to people that are not there. I thought you went to the doctor to get a refill on her medications? Is she not taking them?" Dad asked, now leaning forward in the chair, talking directly to my mom in frustration.

"I did take her to the doctor, John. Dr. Flora refilled her medication, and she brought it up with her to her room. I know she's taking it, John; she has been acting normal," But my mom wasn't able to finish her sentence before my dad cut in.

"Clearly, she's not taking them, Dianna. She is up

there in her room having conversations with herself or someone that we can't see or Jordan can't see. This means she is having delusions, auditory hallucinations, visual hallucinations, hearing voices! Please chime in when this starts to ring a bell, Dianna!" he retorted.

"She was on her medications when the shooting happened, John. That was right about the time when she ran out of them, though. But she was on them. Jennifer even told me she was out of them and she needed more. Clearly, she was lucid enough to know she was out and needed more," she pleaded in defense.

"Dianna! Jennifer was diagnosed with schizophrenia! She hears voices and sees people that are not really there! She hallucinates constantly! Jordan just heard her talking to herself in her room! Those are called delusions and auditory hallucinations," Dad continued to raise his voice, trying to make his point.

"She doesn't remember the shooting; that's why she hasn't brought it up, been distraught, depressed, or even expressed any type of shock. She is living in her own world. Jennifer is acting like one of the biggest mass shootings in history never even happened," he threw his hands up in the air.

His anger took my mom and sister off guard. My dad was stern, but it took a lot for him to get as angry as he was. They both were speechless. I laid down in the hallway, continuing to eavesdrop on the conversation. I could not believe what my family was saying about me. I felt like they were against me, mad at me, and constantly a burden to all of them. I wanted to start crying again, but I held it back. I could not let any of them hear me.

"She was on her pills for three months before the shooting, and she was on them when it happened, and," Mom tried to gather what she was going to say next. "Then she ran out the day after the shooting. Yes, I agree with you. She was completely lucid the day of the shooting. Then she ran out of her pills, which might have been when she started to detach from reality again, just like when she was first diagnosed," her voice very shaken now.

"Great, so she has the pills, but she's not taking them, Dianna. Jennifer just proved that to us, well, Jordan did," Dad said, in a calmer manner, raising his hand toward the stairs.

"I'll go up there and talk to her, John. I'll grab her pills, and we will see how many she has taken. Just so you know, it does sometimes take a while to kick in, especially when she was off of them for five days or more," she sighed.

My mom started up the stairs. She squeezed past my sister, who was still sitting on the stairway. I was still lying in the hallway, but as soon as my mom's back turned away from me, I quickly got up and crawled towards my door. I opened it, quickly crawling through it. I shut the door quietly, just in time for my mom to start walking down the hallway. I stood up and ran towards my desk.

I opened up the pill bottle and took four pills out of the bottle, and threw them in my nightstand. I left the pill bottle on my desk and sat on my bed. I grabbed my backpack and started pulling out textbooks. I heard the footsteps of my mom getting closer to my door. I looked towards the as my mom started to knock.

"She's opening the door. She's coming in here, and you better tell her nothing happened," The Unknown Male voice said.

"Hey Jenn, can I talk to you for a second?" Mom asked as she sat on my bed.

"Yeah, Mom. What's going on? Is everything okay?" I asked.

"Okay, well, I am just going to get straight to the point. Have you been taking your pills, Jenn? I want you to be honest with me." She asked.

"Yes, I have. As soon as I got them refilled, I started retaking them, and I wasn't off of them for that long," I said as convincingly as possible.

"Can I see your pill bottle?" she asked as she stared over at my desk.

At this point, I could not object. Mom went towards my desk and grabbed the pill bottle, noticing pills were gone. She held the pill bottle and then looked at me, and I just looked back at her with all the confidence I could conjure. My mom then smiled while walking towards the edge of my bed.

"You have been acting very strange, Jenn. You're withdrawn, you don't talk to anyone, you only come down from your room to eat dinner, and you have barely touched your homework. Your grades are slipping, some of your teachers have called us. They say you're not participating or completing assignments. It makes me question if you're taking your medication like Dr. Flora had said to do.

Otherwise, Jenn, you begin to see and hear things that are not real. You do understand that don't you? You're schizophrenic, Jennifer," she explained. I was not comprehending what she was saying. I nodded my head and repeatedly said, I know. I rarely made eye contact with her as she was talking to me.

"Well, I have been taking them, and everything is fine. I will try to be more social, do better in classes, and get my homework done. I realize I have not been doing well in that department," I defended myself in the calmest manner I could.

She got up from my bed and gave me a hug. The hug felt so warm and comforting. My mom wanted to be there for me; she wanted me to be okay. I hated that my family was talking about me behind my back, though. My mom then walked out of my room. She gave me the usual look of hope and consistency, which was a look I could never forget. I saw the door close behind her.

The footsteps faded down the hallway and then down the stairs. This time I did not open my door again. I stayed seated on my bed, staring at the pill bottle. I walked over to the desk, grabbed the pill

91

bottle, grasping it very tightly. I was beginning to contemplate taking the pills.

"Don't do it, Jenn. You need us. You need us," The Male voice said.

I shook my head and grabbed my hair. I put my hands over my eyes with the pill bottle still in my hand.

"Don't take it. You will lose me. You need me, and you will find that out soon enough, I promise," The Female voice said.

I opened my eyes and set the pill bottle back down on my desk. I sat back on my bed and picked up my textbook, flipping through the pages. My mom was right; I needed to start getting my homework done and doing better in school.

"I'll give you the answers. I know the information." The Male voice said.

I held my math book, then stared at my closet. My eyes blinked slowly as a tear fell from my face.

CHAPTER 15
DECISIONS

I put the pill bottle down on my nightstand. I read the label over and over again. It read, *Clozapine*. I stared at it, as if the words were going to change, or maybe I was not seeing the words correctly.

"You don't want to take something not knowing what it is." The Male voice said.

I turned my attention to my math book. I flipped to the page that we left off at in class. I started reading and writing the problems down in my notebook. I had to look back and forth. From my textbook and back to my notebook. I wrote down a problem and I could not figure out how to solve it.

"You have to isolate the X factor and then divide on both sides." The Female voice said, as if she was sitting right next to me helping me with my homework.

I started working on the problem. It all started to come back to me. I felt like I knew what I was doing. I decided to check the answer at the back of the book just to make sure I had the right answer. I did, I was exhilarated. I was actually able to work on a problem without any problems. I worked on a couple more problems as the voices came to help, as they always seemed to do. They gave me the answers, but I still checked them in the back of the book.

After about an hour, I looked at my clock to see that it was 10 in the evening. It was getting late. I closed my text book and notebook. I stuffed them back into my backpack. I went in to the bathroom to brush my teeth. Later throwing on my pajama pants and an old short sleeve shirt. I pulled my covers out, turned out the light, and laid down.

"Are you really tired? You don't look tired." The Female voice said.

"She's laying down." The Male voice continued as the voices started overlapped each other.

I sat up and turned on the light on the night stand. I started to breathe heavily. I was getting frustrated. My attention then turned to the desk where my pills were. I pulled the covers off and took the pills in my hand. I sighed, as I opened the bottle. I took one of the pills out, got some water, and took the pill. I set my water and pills back on the desk and crawled into bed.

I stared at the ceiling, then realized I was dreadfully uncomfortable. I could still hear all of the voices talking about me as they watched me try to fall asleep. The voices became so loud that I attempted tuning it out by turning to my side and slamming my pillow over my head, and my arm over the pillow. I finally started to feel like I was falling asleep.

"I wanted to kill everyone and that's what I did. I am going to kill you and there's nothing you can do to stop me." Derek said, in the most hateful tone I had ever heard.

"You don't have to do this, Derek. I know you weren't fit for this world and neither am I, okay? I am just like you. I know how you feel." I said, trying to be empathetic.

"You have no fucking idea how I feel! You don't know me!" Derek screamed.

"Really? I don't know you? What about all those times at the park? You held my hand. You fucking kissed me? I am the only person you can talk to and you opened up to me. God!" I started to cry. "Now your acting like I am your first target. After everything we talked about," I said, wiping my eyes.

"I really don't care how you feel, nor the pain I am going to inflict on you. I don't feel sorry for you! I have no mercy for anyone, not even you," he said more calmly. His hair began to fly over his eyes once again. I looked around to notice we were back at the park sitting at the table under the gazebo. It was foggy and rainy. I could not believe what I was hearing and I stood up from the table.

I started to cry. I did not want to, but I couldn't

help it. I looked up at Derek with tears running down my face. I started to cover my eyes. Just as I took my hand down, Derek was right back up in my face. I took a step back, but he grabbed me and pulled me towards him. I was frightened as Derek became more unpredictable and hostile.

"You are already dead. You are dead at my hands. Do you understand me? As Derek held me tightly and looked directly into my eyes. That was the first time I noticed that I could not see my reflection in his eyes. His eyes were truly dead. I realized there was nothing I could do to save Derek. He has already made up his mind. *Maybe I was already dead and had not realized it...*

"Derek let go of me," I yelled, pulling away. "If you want to kill me so fucking bad then do it! C'mon do it! I don't know what I did to you or how I wronged you, but it's obvious that you want me dead, so just kill me. Believe me when I say my life is a living hell!" I screamed at him. Derek looked away from me. I started to calm down and hold my ground. "You can't do it can you? I would have already been dead by now, but I am not." I stood there with confidence.

Derek turned back around at me. He did not smile, but looked at me like he had won a fight. At that moment, I felt like I could see everything that Derek had done. *He methodically planned a mass shooting to take place at our school. He had what he needed, the guns, the ammo, the time, and the place. Derek was able to fool everyone that he was a social outcast, and yet a good student. However, no one*

could see the evil that was locked inside. He fooled
everyone; including myself, until now.

CHAPTER 16
AWAKEN

I woke up gasping for air, panting, and holding my chest. I realized I was crying and sweating and put my face to my knees while still under the covers. I looked up; I covered my mouth, trying not to scream. I was trying to stay as quiet as possible, trying not to wake anyone up. The dream was so vivid. I tried to calm myself down, but that was easier said than done. I got out from under the covers and sat on the bed with my hands still on my face.

"Calm down, Jenn. It's fine. It was just a dream. Nothing to worry about. Get it together," I said aloud as I tried to slow down my breathing. I began to shake my hands, trying to calm myself. I looked over at my alarm clock that read 5:30 in the morning. I took a deep breath. I had a little time to spare before I had to start getting ready for school.

Math was my first period. It occurred to me that I had not done my homework last night. I looked down at my backpack sitting beside my bed. I pulled the textbook out with my notebook. I opened up my math book to where we left off in class. I then opened up my notebook to see that my homework had been done. I was confused. I looked again at the notebook; all the problems that had been assigned were done. I could not remember completing the assignment. I stared at my notebook, flipping through the pages. I grabbed my textbook and flipped through the pages all the way to the back. All of the answers that I had written in my notebook were right, and they matched the textbook. There was no way I did this by myself. I am terrible at math. I dropped my notebook on the bed, then stepped away from it. I looked back and forth between the textbook and the notebook. Trying to retrace last night's events. *When did I do this?*

I walked over to the window to open the blinds to check the weather. I could feel the cold coming off of the window pane. It was raining and foggy. Again. I went to the closet and grabbed a hoodie, jeans, and some shoes. As I put on the hoodie, I realized that I had already worn this one about a week and a half ago. It is the only black with white hood strings hoodie that I have. But it smelled like it was freshly washed. The same with the jeans, also recently worn – and again freshly washed.

What in the world was going on here? My math homework was done, and my clothes were just cleaned. I was positive that I had already worn that hoodie; I was sure of it.

I was running out of time. I hurried up, threw on my clothes, brushed my hair, and brushed my teeth. I grabbed my backpack and went down the hallway. As I was walked past my sister's room, I realized I had forgotten to grab one of my pills to take before heading out. I sighed and went back to my room. I grabbed the pills off the desk and opened them. There were only two pills left? *I thought I had more?* I took one of the pills, went down the hallway and down the stairs.

I came downstairs to see my mom in the kitchen in her bathrobe, drinking coffee. Jordan was sitting at the table. She had on an outrageous outfit. Makeup was done, skinny jeans on, and a tight top. I went into the kitchen to get some coffee. As I went to the refrigerator with my coffee cup to get some creamer, I glanced at the calendar. I took a step back in shock, gasped, and accidentally dropped my coffee mug on the floor. My mom came rushing into the kitchen.

"Mom! What day is it today? What the hell is that? As I pointed towards the calendar.

"Jennifer! There's glass everywhere. Let me go get a broom, and you get some paper towels. Please start cleaning this up; you are going to be late," Mom said irritably.

"No, Mom, please come here. Please! What is today? Why is the calendar still in August?" I sputtered. I started bouncing around as if I had to go to the bathroom.

"Jennifer, calm down. The calendar says August because it's August. August 29th, to be exact. I have to start pulling out my fall decorations. I will probably do that today," Mom continued to ramble.

"No, wait, it's supposed to be September 15th or

100

something like that, right?" I asked, waiting impatiently for an answer and still pointing at the calendar.

"Jennifer, it's August 29th, okay? It's not a big deal. I know you're bummed that you just went back to school, and it's stressful," Mom said, trying to clean up the glass and coffee.

"No, it's not like that, Mom," I continued as she interrupted me.

"I am telling you we are at the end of August," She told me once again with a wet coffee paper towel in her hand.

"Oh my god. Oh, holy hell! Are you serious right now?" speaking to myself. I had lost track of time, but how? How is it, August? It already passed. Was I delusional?

"Jenn, you have been taking your medication, right?" She asked with concern in her voice as she dumped the pieces of the coffee mug in the trash.

I looked back at her, not knowing what to say.

CHAPTER 17
THE END OF AUGUST

I looked at my mom with shock. I could not believe what was happening. "Yeah, I just took it this morning, but I am running out, and I need a refill. I just wanted to let you know before I forgot. Umm… that's why I was so surprised. Sorry, I didn't mean to make you worry." I continued to ramble and tried to explain myself. "I'll be right back. I forgot something upstairs." I stood there for a few seconds, then turned and walked up the stairs.

I hurried up the stairs and down the hallway to my room. I quickly went straight to the calendar on the desk. August 29th! I flipped the page over to see September, then flipped back to August. I scanned it, once again, to September, then back again to August. It finally dawned on me that it would not change the date no matter how many times I flipped the page. I took a deep breath, put my arms on my head, and tried to make sense of everything. *What the hell is going on?* I had no choice but to go with it. I grabbed the pill bottle to give to my mom and went back down the stairs.

Mom and Jordan were waiting at the bottom of the stairs. I said nothing as I handed my mom the bottle, and she placed it on the counter.

"Okay, I'm going to go to school now," I said, heading for the front door.

"Jenn, don't forget your backpack," Mom called, pointing to my backpack.

"Right. Yeah, and that might help," I said as I stumbled over my words.

I grabbed my backpack on the floor near the kitchen counter. I started toward the front door. This time, I did not look back at my mom or sister. I went out the front door and closed it behind me. I stood outside. It was definitely colder than it looked from my bedroom window. I pulled the hood over my head and started walking.

The leaves on the sidewalk were damp with rain. *I love the fall, except when I had to walk to school in the rain. Again.* I could feel the mist of rain on my face as I walked. The sidewalk made its gentle uphill grade towards school. I looked around at the houses as I passed by. Their lights were haloed by the fog. Silhouettes of people preparing for their day reflected on the windows. Condensation collected on the cars that lined the streets and driveways.

The walk to school seemed like it was taking forever, and I decided I would try and cut the walk in half. At the top of the hill, I turned into the other neighborhood in the community. There was a shortcut through there. I would have to walk by the elementary school, but the rain was freezing, and cutting through the little kids would be worth it. *I really liked this weather, but it was far better to sit on the couch with a blanket.*

I made it through the second neighborhood. I looked down at my feet and noticed how many leaves were stuck to my shoes. I stopped to brush the leaves off. I looked up to see the elementary school. I walked towards the elementary school and the path that leads to King High School. I had to cross a small field to get to the other sidewalk. There was a pavilion and playground just before the path to my school.

I reached the pavilion. I was getting close to school. I tried stomping my feet on the concrete to get the leaves off my shoes, but that didn't seem to work. As I passed the pavilion, a dark and cold feeling rushed over me. It stopped me in my tracks. I stood staring at the gazebo and swings swaying in the wind. I wiped the rain and moved the hair from my face. My breathing and heart rate were elevated. For some reason, the sight of this gazebo filled me with anxiety. No one else was here.

The swings were dripping wet. The mulch at the playground was darkened in color from the rain. The four tables beneath the gazebo were the only things untouched by the rain. I stood under the pavilion, my gaze drawn to the swings. I walked over to the swing set. I pushed one of the swings; beads of water came crashing down. I watched the water drip from my hand to my fingertips. I then looked up to barely see my high school in the distance through the mist and fog. I was suddenly filled with despair. I didn't know where this feeling was coming from.

I looked back at the water dripping from the chain of the swing. I held my hand under the swing and let it fill with water. I stared at it for a moment; its chill felt familiar. I allow the water to run out onto the mulch below. I looked back towards the gazebo, water running down its roof and onto the concrete below. It was so quiet...

I felt like I was in a trance like I was stuck in a moment. A moment that I thought I had experienced before. But, when? The swing started to sway in the wind; its gentle squeal broke the silence and brought me back to myself. I shook my head and took my phone from my pocket to see what time it was. I had been standing here for thirty minutes! I needed to get going. I turned away from the park and started down the sidewalk to school.

As I approached the school, I could hear chatter from the kids outside, desperately trying to get out of the rain and into the school. Everyone was happy, hugging each other hello, talking on cell phones, and getting ready for class. I hurried up the steps of the high school to get out of the rain. I took off my hood and did my best to dry it off. I looked around to see kids at their lockers, getting their books, teachers conversing with one another before they started towards their class, a typical day at school.

As I walked to my locker, I looked to my left to

105

see the popular Dianna and Casey. They looked beautiful as always. Not far from them was always a group of popular football and basketball players. Alex was the quarterback of the football team and Dianna's boyfriend, tall and muscular. He had short brown hair and blue eyes. Believe it or not, I always thought those two looked good together. Albeit cliché, at the same time.

Casey also dated a football player, and Darren was a wide receiver. He looked like Alex, but he had long hair, and he was a little bit shorter.

The school was filled with happy chatter and the usual gossip. Everyone seemed to be glad to be at school, except me.

I finally got to my locker, used the combination to open it. I put my wet backpack inside, took out my math book and notebook. The one thing I was happy about was that I finished my math homework. For once, I was prepared for class, which actually perked me up a little bit. I got all my supplies together.

Fighting and laughing broke down the hall. That usually only meant one thing. Someone was getting picked on. I peeked around my locker to see what was happening. The football players had circled around one of the students.

It was Derek Kretin.

CHAPTER 18
LAST CHANCE

Suddenly, I started getting flashbacks of Derek. The pavilion, the swing set, the tables. The black jacket, blue jeans, and black gloves. Derek. Derek's hair; always in his eyes. The cold dark stare he gave me. It all came over me like a massive rush of adrenaline. I could not control my thoughts. It all happened so fast. My heart rate and breathing sped up as if I had been running a marathon. I quickly moved my damp hair away from my face and hurried toward the circle of jocks. I had no idea what I was doing or what had come over me. I knew I had to stop it. I got to one of the football players. I tried to pull him off of Derek, who he had pinned against the lockers with my strength.

"Stop! Stop it!" I shouted as I tried to pull one of the many football players off of Derek. "What the hell are you doing? What did he ever do to you?" I shouted towards everyone, standing in front of Derek.

Everyone stopped and looked at me. They all

started to laugh and cock their heads with arrogance. I looked back at Derek, who was still up against the lockers, his nose bleeding. The blood dripped down his face, then to his mouth, and onto his faded green shirt. He started to wipe his face and then looked at the blood on his hand. I looked back at the six football players surrounding Derek and me. My face was filled with rage.

"First of all, who the hell are you? Do you even go to this school?" one of the football players asked me as he stepped in front of the others.

I did not answer back. I just looked at him, still standing in front of Derek.

"Yeah, man, she does go to this school. She's the crazy girl, remember?" He said as he looked at the other football players in the circle.

I looked at the next football player that started to talk. I had no words but just shook my head slowly. I looked to my left to see the school resource officer and teachers were headed our way.

"What the hell is going on here? Someone better start talking right now!" Officer Smith demanded as he stood there, with his hands on his hips. Nobody said a word. I looked at the school resource officer, as did everyone else while the group was dispersing. I kept standing close to Derek; later, I turned to face him and then backed away. I saw the blood pouring from his nose and his lip.

"Here, let's get you to the nurse, okay?" Officer

Smith said, reaching for Derek's arm.

"Just leave me alone! I'm fine. It's nothing I can't handle, okay?" he said as he grabbed his backpack from the floor.

I looked at Derek and then Officer Smith and then back at Derek.

"Okay, but at least go to the bathroom, and wash your face before you go to class." Officer Smith said to Derek as he walked towards the bathroom. "I suggest you get to class too, young lady," he said as he pointed down the hall. I looked down the hall, then back at Officer Smith.

I nodded my head, picked up my backpack, and walked towards my locker. I looked back and saw that Officer Smith, as well as the other two teachers, had turned the corner. They could no longer see me. Instead of going to class, I decided to follow Derek, as anything school-related was the last place he would go.

I waited around the corner near the boy's bathroom. There was a brick wall I could easily conceal myself behind. I heard the bathroom door open, and Derek walked out. I took a step back, now leaning against the brick wall, making sure that Derek would not see me. He was heading for the front door of the school. I watched him walk down the hallway. His faded green shirt, jeans, and black shoes slowly faded into a silhouette as he walked into the daylight outside the school.

I watched him from a distance until he was out of sight. I dropped my backpack and hurried to the front of the school, trying to catch up with him. I reached the entrance, Derek was nowhere to be found. I looked both ways, scanning each end of the parking lot, but could not see him. I did not know what came over me. I was not that person who stopped fights at school.

I walked back into the school. The hallway was deserted; everyone was in class except me. I picked up my backpack and went to math class, and I was going to draw attention to myself by being late. I peeked through the narrow window of the classroom; the teacher was in front of the class giving a lecture. I opened the door, all eyes were on me. The teacher shook her head and pointed towards my desk. I sat down and pulled out my books.

"I take it you don't have your homework done, Jennifer?" my teacher said to me, as I quickly looked up at her.

"No, actually, I do have it done. Here it is," I replied as I handed her the assignment.

She took it from me, looked at it, and said nothing more. I gave a sigh of relief and leaned back in my chair. My teacher continued with her lecture. I glanced around the class; Lacy was sitting behind me. I smiled at her, and she gave a slight wave to me. "After class, we have to talk," Lacy whispered to me. I nodded my head and faced forward.

After about an hour and fifteen minutes, the bell

110

rang. Everyone was dispersing from the classroom as I quickly gathered my things and stuffed them in my backpack. Lacy grabbed my arm and walked out the door with me.

"Hey, Jenn! It's been a while! I've missed you! I haven't talked to you in forever!" she said, giving me a big hug.

"What are you talking about? I called you a couple days ago, but you really didn't say much," I replied.

"No, you didn't, Jenn. Okay, listen - as your best friend - you have been really out of it. You had to stay home from school for a while. You don't remember?" she said as we stopped in the middle of the hallway. "I was at home? Are you sure?" I asked in complete disbelief.

"Yeah, I mean, that's what your mom said. You ran out of your medication, and well, you weren't yourself for like two weeks until you got back on them, and now you're here; you're the same Jenn, my best friend," she hugged me once more. "Can we stop and talk about what came over you before school? I have never seen you step in and stop a fight like that! I mean, that was brilliant and so confident. You actually stood in front of six football players and protected Derek! I can't get over this," she continued to ramble on as she practically dragged me down the hall with her arm wrapped around mine. I soon stopped walking with Lacy still holding my arm.

"Lacy, as my best friend, can you tell me what happens to me when I'm off my medication? Please, I need to know. I am constantly in a fog and really don't know what happens. It's like I blackout or something." I asked, standing right in front of her. Lacy stood there for a second, looking at me with sorrow.

Lacy let go of my arm and stood in front of me. She looked around at our classmates passing by, then looked back at me. She was going to tell me, and I was ready to listen.

CHAPTER 19
THE TRUTH

Lacy stayed silent for what felt like forever as I waited for an answer.

"Okay, Jenn, when you're off your medication, you're not yourself. You start seeing things, hearing things, talking to yourself, and talking to people that are not there. You were diagnosed with schizophrenia," she explained to me. "You were off your medication for that week. You and I were having a conversation about school. Still, instead of listening to me, you were talking to someone else and answering someone else. You weren't even engaged with the conversation we were having. Still, you were having a conversation with someone else that I couldn't see or hear. Now, when you're on your medication, that doesn't seem to happen. Like right now, you are here, and you're listening to me. You are comprehending what I am saying."

I leaned up against the lockers, turned my head to

the side. I started breathing heavily, my heart started to race. My hands were on top of my head, and I slammed them against the lockers. It startled Lacy, but she did not move.

"Jenn, you go into your own world when you're off your medication. It's like you're not in this reality but in another reality. It's in your own head. Ever since you were diagnosed, I have done a lot of research, and it's a devastating disease. Still, everything is in your head, and it's not reality," she said as she stood in front of me, desperately trying to get me to understand. But I understood. Perfectly.

"Okay, so when I am off my medication, I start hearing things and seeing things, right?" I asked, waiting for confirmation.

"Yes, that's right," she sighed.

"Okay, I know what I have to do now," I walked away from Lacy and hurried down the hall. Lacy darted after me, then grabbed my arm, and I quickly pulled it away.

"Wait! What the hell? What do you have to do?" Lacy asked desperately.

"I need to get off this medication and go back into my own reality," I stood and faced her.

"Okay, umm, may I ask why!? Why would you want to do something like that? You're finally back to normal, talking to me and other people, somewhat, I guess." Lacy shot back, throwing her hands in frustration.

"Lacy, something is going to happen. I don't know what, but it's something bad. I am going to sound crazier than I already sound. But I don't know what is going to happen until I am off of this medication. I know this because I have been having crazy flashbacks with Derek. Filled with sorrow and dread." I took a deep breath.

"I might have been in my own world, or 'reality,' whatever you want to call it, but there's an answer there, and I need to go back and find it. I can't do that when my brain is locked up on this medication. You are my best friend, you told me the truth, it's what I needed to hear, and now that I have heard it, I know what I have to do. This is a sick and horrible curse, but I guess that's why it's called a curse because you don't have a choice in the matter. Now I do, thanks to you, I am making that choice right now," I stood looking to her for acceptance.

"Wait! Derek? What does Derek have to do with any of this? Do you like him or something?" she asked with confusion.

"Oh my God, no, Lacy!" I said, trying not to get mad at her. I felt that was far from the truth but could not explain it. "I need to go. You need to let me go right now," I said reassuringly. "Trust me on this, but when I come back tomorrow, just bear with me, okay? If you're talking to me and I start talking to someone else, please don't take it personally, okay? Once I find what I am looking for, you will know, okay, Lacy?" as I gently reached for her arm.

Lacy nodded; I started to see tears in her eyes.

115

Lacy hugged me, then pushed me back slightly, assuring me I had her blessing. I pushed open the front door, and I did not look back. My mind was clear.

I went down the steps, only to run right into Officer Smith.

"Don't you have your second class to get to, Jennifer?" Officer Smith asked, backing up at the same time.

"Oh no, I actually feel really sick. I need to go home," I said, hunching over.

"Did you go to the nurse? Are you going to be okay?" He asked with concern.

"Yeah, I went to the nurse. I'm sure I'll be fine; I just really need to go home." Looking extremely desperate.

"Okay, I'll see you tomorrow. I hope you feel better." Officer Smith said as I turned away, walking through the parking lot.

It was going to be a long walk home. I ran through the parking lot as soon as Officer Smith was out of sight. The rain was heavier, the fog was thicker, I could barely see through both. The rain was hitting my face like sheets of ice. I could hear the water sloshing beneath my feet as I ran, even more so when I hit the grass. I passed that pavilion and playground. I thought I saw a figure as I glanced at it but kept running.

Suddenly, I was at the top of the hill to where my neighborhood started. It was all downhill from here. The rain was heavier. The fog looked thicker as it hovered over the bottom of the hill. I reached the end of the cul-de-sac, stopping to catch my breath. I started walking home, looking around to see that all of the cars I had seen this morning were now gone. Deserted, again. I got to my front door. I walked in soaking wet and went straight upstairs. No one was home. I got to my room and immediately changed out of my clothes. I found a piece of paper to make a list of. I started writing:

Lacy knows...

Talk to the principal today...

Look for Derek...

I only wrote down three thoughts, not knowing why or what they really meant. It was a strong feeling, telling me to write it down, though. I stood up from my desk, then sat on my bed. I saw the pill bottle back on my desk. My mom must have put it back up here before she went to work. I grabbed the bottle. I knew I took one right before school, which was only four hours ago. I had a long way to go. I stayed up in my room as long as possible.

I pulled out my phone. There was a text from Lacy. "Did u make it home?"

"Yeah. THX again. See u 2morrow."

"K. Do what u have 2 do. Love u!"

"Love u."

I set my phone down and turned on the TV. There wasn't a lot on during the day, and I could feel myself drifting off to sleep. I suddenly woke up to a knock on the door. I had not dreamt of anything. The knocking continued.

"Yeah, come in," I said, looking at the door, still laying down.

"Jenn, what are you doing home? Are you sick?" Dad asked me.

That was an understatement.

"Yeah, I came home early. I wasn't feeling well," I said to him, trying to look as sick as possible.

"Okay, well, let me know if you need anything. We are all downstairs," Dad said as he shut the door.

"Okay. Thanks, Dad," he closed the door.

I sat up in bed. I looked at the clock to see that it was now eight in the evening. I struggled to wake up. I grabbed my phone to see there were no messages.

"She's setting the phone down." The Unknown Male voice said.

I gasped. I quickly looked up and smiled.

118

CHAPTER 20
NOW OR NEVER

The voices that plagued my life and my brain were back. I was ecstatic! I laid back down, looked toward the closet, still smiling. I was back in my own world, but this time I knew what I was looking for. Everything came back to me as if I had never left. I knew where I wanted to go tomorrow, and that was to the gazebo at the playground. I was going to see Derek, and I would be able to talk to him. Even if he did not want to speak to me. I shot out of bed and went over to my desk to grab the pill bottle. I put it in the desk drawer, hoping my mom would think I had taken it.

"She's putting the pills away." The Female voice said.

"She's going to die. Pills. Die." A more sinister Male voice said.

I shook my head, trying to ignore them. There were going to be consequences to this; I had to remember that. Taking the pills would make the voices go away, but I could not have Derek go away. I

119

laid back down, desperately trying to sleep. I felt myself drifting off to sleep once again but quickly woke back up and looked at my clock. It was 2 in the morning. It felt like I had not slept. There were no dreams, which was disappointing. I was frustrated but did my best to fall asleep again. The next time I woke up, it was 6 in the morning.

"She's waking up." The Female voice said

I quickly sat up in my bed, and I headed for the closet. I threw on my clothes and got ready as fast as I could. I opened up the shades and saw a note on my desk. Which I took and stuffed in my pocket. I grabbed my backpack and took off down the stairs. My family was already up. Mom was drinking coffee in her robe, Jordan looked stunning as usual, and Dad was in his suit getting ready to leave for work.

"Morning, honey! Do you want breakfast, or are you still not feeling well?" Dad asked as I was heading for the door.

"Still not feeling that great, but I'll just grab something at school later," I said, hurrying towards the front door.

"Did you take your medication?" Mom asked, with my back still turned.

"Yep, I took it. I still need that refill, Mom," I said confidently as I grabbed the doorknob.

"You're such a liar!" The Sinister Male voice said.

"Shut up!" I said under my breath.

"What?" Mom asked.

"Nothing, I got to go to school. I am going to be late," I said back quickly and walked out the door.

I took off down the driveway; I walked to the end of the cul-de-sac. It was foggy and rainy. I pulled the hood over my head and started to walk up the hill to school. My walk then turned into a jog, which then turned into a run. I reached the top of the hill. I ran into the next neighborhood. I ran past everything and did not look to see what was around me.

"She's running now," The Female voice said.

I tried to ignore the voices as best as I could. I could see the elementary school, which meant I was getting closer. I kept running and hit the grass. The water on the grass was sloshing, splashing on me as I ran towards the pavilion. My hood flew down off my head. I made it to the pavilion and practically fell over to catch my breath. I looked up, gazing around the playground and gazebo to see that no one was around. I spun around in circles, looking for Derek.

"C'mon, I know you're here," I said out loud. "Damnit, I know you're here. Where are you?" I sat down at the table, still looking around. I put my head down on the table to rest on my hands.

"There he is." The Male voice said.

"Are you looking for me?" Derek said, walking toward me.

121

I quickly jumped and looked around. I immediately looked up from the table, then stood eye to eye with Derek.

"I haven't seen you. Where have you been?" Derek asked as he came closer towards me.

"I need to talk to you," I said to him, trying to remain as calm as possible.

"What about? I'm already dead and correct me if I am wrong, but so are you," he pointed at, giving me a sinister look.

"No! You might be dead, but I am not. I am here, and I am very much alive." I said back, glaring at him.

"Okay, but you won't be for much longer," He said, laughing and walking toward the swing set.

"You can't do this; I'm not going to let you," I said, looking directly at him.

"You're not going to stop me! It's done! You're done!" he said, in a low tone of voice.

"It's not done, and I am definitely not done with any of this." I shot back, pointing my finger at Derek.

"How are you talking to me? Huh? Jennifer, I am dead. You wouldn't be talking to me if I were alive," he quipped as he stood by the swing, grabbing the chain.

"You're not real! You are not real, and you're not dead yet!" I screamed while holding my ground.

"You're going to die," The Male voice said.

I was feeling overwhelmed. There were too many voices talking to me; it felt different because I knew them now. I started walking away from Derek, and I looked back to see that he was starting to follow me.

"Where are you going?" Derek asked as he tried to catch up with me.

"Your dead remember? You figure it out," I shot back as I turned toward the school, trying to see it through the fog and mist.

"Listen, I like you, Jenn. You are the only one I can talk to, and I know you like me too. If you didn't, then why did you help me? Why did you stop that fight?" he pleaded. I stopped dead in my tracks, turned around, and glared at him.

"Why in the hell would I help you?" I demanded as I turned my head to the side, demanding an answer.

"You stopped the fight. You stopped me from getting beat up. Don't you remember?" Derek asked more calmly and sweetly.

I suddenly had a flashback. I saw Lacy, the teachers, and Officer Smith. All of a sudden, I could hear myself screaming, "Stop! Stop it!" I was standing in front of Derek. There was blood. There was blood dripping from his nose, and his lip was busted. I came back to my senses. *I guess that's what being on and off the medication does in a short period. I can go from reality back to my "reality."*

I remembered. I focused on Derek; I strolled toward him on the sidewalk. I stood face to face with him. I began to scan him up and down. Right now, he was wearing his black jacket, jeans, gloves, and black combat boots. His hair was covering one eye as it swayed in the wind. I looked at his nose and lips to see that they were not bleeding. This was not real. Derek was not honest. Derek then started to reach for my arm; I quickly pulled away. I started towards the school, shaking my head.

"No one is going to believe you, Jenn." The Male voice said.

"I don't care. I have to try," I said back out loud.

"Everyone knows you're sick, Jennifer. It already happened. You just don't know it yet, but you will. I promise." Derek said, as his voice started to fade the further I walked away from him. I looked back. Derek was gone. I pulled the hood back up over my head and hurried towards the school. I pulled out the list that I had stuffed in my pocket. "Talk to the principal." That is where I was headed.

124

CHAPTER 21
END OF THE LINE

I reached the school. I stood in the parking lot for a little bit and started looking around. I fog was haloing the school and parking lot. I swiftly walked up the steps to get to the front entrance. I pulled the door open to see Ben standing there.

"Hey Jenn, how's it going? You're here early. Are you finished with your assignment? It's due today." Ben asked as he followed me down the hall. "Yeah, I might have. For what class? When is it due?" I looked at him, still walking fast.

"For world history. You know! We had to write about the King of our choice in Europe in the year 1693. It's September 1st; it's due today." Ben said, as I stopped, once again.

"What? Is it September 1st? Today? Oh my God, I skipped two whole days. I don't remember that." I said under my breath.

Another flashback started to happen. I could hear Derek talking about the shooting and myself asking Derek what day this had happened. Derek said it was September 1st. I asked him if it was this year or last year, and he couldn't remember. My breathing began to elevate, my heart began to race once more. I put my hand over my mouth, I started to panic.

"Ben, have you seen Derek?" I asked quickly. "Derek who? There's more than one." He said back to me, smiling.

"Kretin, Ben! Derek Kretin! Where is he?" I shouted.

Ben was taken aback. He stood there puzzled.

"I haven't seen him yet. He went home early a day ago maybe, but I didn't see him again. Why? What's going on?" Ben asked as I turned away from him and hurried toward the principal's office.

I did not answer Ben. I kept heading towards the principal's office, and I had to get there now! I started to jog down the hallway.

"Jenn! Jenn! What is going on?" he shouted as he jogged alongside me.

I could not answer Ben. As I was jogging, I could see all my fellow classmates fly past me, looking at me with confusion. I finally made it to the principal's office. I ripped open the door; Ben was still behind me. Everyone in the office was looking at me. I could see the look on their faces. They wanted to know what was going on.

"I need to speak with Principal Vaughn, and it's urgent," I stood near the doorway of the office, trying to get the hair out of my face. I could see that Ben was still standing behind me; he wanted an answer from me just as much as everyone else in the office. The three ladies in the office didn't say anything, but one lady got up and knocked on Principal Vaughn's door.

"Ben, I think you should just go; as a matter of fact, you should go home. I am being serious," I said as I turned around to face him.

"No way, I want to hear what you have to say," he said with interest.

I gave up and sat in one of the four empty chairs in the office. My feet and legs started to shake anxiously, and I wanted Principal Vaughn to come out of his office already. Finally, I heard the door open, looked up, and Principal Vaughn went out of his office. I stood up as quick as I could, with Ben mimicking my every movement.

"Jennifer, what is going on? Why aren't you in class?" asked Principal Vaughn, still standing behind the main office desk.

"I need to talk to you. It's going to sound crazy, but I need you to listen to me." I demanded as I stood at the front desk, now leaning over it. "Okay, come into my office." He said as he held the door.

"I am coming too," Ben said, still following me.

I could tell Principal Vaughn did not want Ben in the office, but at this point, he knew he didn't have a choice. Ben and I sat down while Principal Vaughn sat behind his desk. Ben then stood up, and I could tell he was anxious.

"Look, I know this is going to sound crazy, but Derek Kretin is going to shoot up the school!" I blurted out, leaning forward in my chair. Ben gave me a look of shock, then looked at Principal Vaughn.

"You know this how?" he asked, folding his hands upon his desk.

"I just know, okay? You have to believe me; this is not a joke," I pleaded as I started to raise my voice, still leaning forward in my chair.

"How? How do you know this? This is a pretty big accusation, Jennifer. You're not giving me any reason to believe that this is true," Principal Vaughn began to speak with his hands. "Did Derek say something to you? Did he tell you he was going to shoot up the school?"

"Yes, as a matter of fact, he did speak to me. He told me he shot up the school, and a lot of people died," I replied as my breathing started to elevate. "He told you 'he shot up the school?' As in past tense?" Principal Vaughn looked at me with doubt. "Look, Jennifer, I know that you were diagnosed with schizophrenia. Maybe this was just a dream you were having. A dream is not real. I know you have been struggling for the past couple of weeks. Still, there's no evidence pointing towards Derek that suggests that he is going to commit mass murder," he said as he leaned back in his chair and folded his hands on his lap.

Principal Vaughn sighed. He continued to look at me with disbelief and worry. Now, he was deciding to humor me. "When is this shooting supposed to happen, Jennifer?"

"No one believes you, Jennifer. You're crazy, and you're going to die," The Male voice said. I shook my head, trying to rid the voice in my head. Principal Vaughn looked, again, at me with doubt and frustration. He did not believe me. Why would he believe me? I was the crazy girl, and God only knows what stories I would make up. I stood up, standing over Principal Vaughn.

"The shooting is going to happen today. I don't know when, but it will happen. You can choose to believe me or not. Call it suspicion or a delusion, but I know it's going to happen. I'm here to try and help save as many people as I can by giving you a warning!" I screamed as I slammed my hands down on his desk.

Principal Vaughn said nothing. Ben sat in his chair in shock. I stood and looked at the clock to see it was 8 in the morning. I looked at Principal Vaughn, he picked up his desk phone. He looked concerned now, and I was relieved. Maybe he was going to try and call a few people to start evacuating the school. "Yes, this is Principal Vaughn. I need you to put the school on lock..." as Principal Vaughn stopped talking, multiple gunshots started to ring out in the

129

distance.

I gasped and covered my mouth. I looked at Principal Vaughn, then at Ben as he had his mouth wide open and looked at the main office door. The phone slowly fell from Principal Vaughn's ear, and he looked at me as fear and realization washed over him. "I told you! It's starting." I said as I stood in front of Principal Vaughn across from his desk. I looked back at Ben; he looked terrified.

"We need to get out of here. We need to get out of here. Right now," I said as multiple gunshots and screaming came from the distance.

Principal Vaughn and Ben nodded as they looked at me.

"This is it," I said to myself, looking at the closed door.

"DIE, JENNIFER," THE MALE VOICE SAID.

CHAPTER 22
REALITY

I ripped open the main office door, grabbed Ben's hand, and ran out the door. Before the door could close, I looked back at Principal Vaughn and the other ladies in the main office.

"You need to get out. Get out of the school!" I shouted at them and turned away.

I looked both ways down the hallway. I could still hear gunshots all around me, but I tried to figure out where they were coming from. Everything was so loud, and I could not make out where Derek was at that moment in time.

"What do we do?" Ben asked frantically, still gripping my hand.

"This way! Down here!" I said as I started to pull Ben down to my right. Fire alarms began to sound.

"He's going to get you, Jennifer." The Female

voice said.

"Run, Jennifer." The Male voice said.

We continued to sprint down the hallway. Suddenly, something made me stop. Ben continued to run past me; he stopped looking back at me with confusion and terror. I pulled out the piece of paper from my hoodie; I *had to find Lacy*. I looked up at Ben, then ran to a stairway that led down to the school's first floor. Ben followed me without saying a word. I ran down the steps, then turned to go down another set of steps.

It was a struggle to keep my footing. I reached the bottom to see at least seven bodies covered with blood. I was still hearing gunshots and screaming; it was getting louder. I put a hand over my mouth and looked around in complete terror and disbelief. Ben looked like he was going to faint. I tried to hold myself together, then grabbed Ben and put him against the wall in the hallway.

"Ben, we need to find Lacy! We need to find her!" I started pulling him again down the hall, and Ben just nodded with tears in his eyes and followed my lead.

We continued to run down the hallway. I kept looking around. Students were running everywhere, frantic; some were hiding in classrooms. Others were trying to get out of the school. I went down another hallway; I saw more students lying there with gunshot wounds to their heads and torsos. Some were leaning up against the lockers, some were lying face down.

132

More gunshots could be heard; they were getting louder. That's when I heard laughing and taunting. *I knew that voice; I knew that laugh.* It was Derek. I wanted to turn around and go back the other way, but I was determined to find Lacy. Ben had a death grip on my hand as we tried to dodge the bodies that were sprawled out on the school floor. There were puddles of blood everywhere, total chaos, and there was nothing I could do to stop it.

I heard splashing under my feet. This time it was not water from the rain under my feet; it was blood. I felt like I was going to be sick. I kept shutting my eyes as we ran down the hallway, wishing that this was another reality, but it was not. This was the true reality; it was happening now and not in my head.

"Go this way, Jennifer!" The Male voice said.

"He won't find you here," The Female voice said tauntingly.

More gunshots, more screaming, and more laughing could be heard, but this time not in the distance. The chaos was close. I stopped running on the sight was my science room. I threw my body against the door to open it. I went in, Ben still holding my hand tightly. I looked around to see at least fifteen students shot dead. Some students were still in their seats, slumped over their textbooks, eyes wide open, and notebook paper drenched with blood. Others had fallen out of their seats, laying on the floor in each other's blood. It looked like a horror movie. I could not believe this was happening.

Ben started to cry; he tried to shut his eyes. I looked at him, then looked all around me. I was surrounded by death and horror, to which I could not say a word. I stood there, motionless and speechless.

More gunshots rang out; it made me come to my senses. I took Ben's hand once more. I shoved the other door of the classroom open. I looked to my left to see one of the school's exits with the daylight outside shining hope. As I gripped Ben's hand to sprint toward the exit, Derek appeared right before the door. He was wearing a black jacket, jeans, black gloves, and black combat boots. *Just as I remembered.* Derek had the assault rifle in his hand as he stood between us and the way out. That path could not be taken.

"Found you!" The Male voice said.

He raised the barrel towards us. I grabbed Ben's hand and threw him to the locker as I heard two bullets go by our heads. Neither one of us was hit.

"Ben, hurry! Let's go!" I grabbed him and headed the opposite way of Derek.

We sprinted down the hall. More gunshots were being fired at us. All I could hear was the sound of my heavy breathing, gunshots, and ringing in my ears. I turned down another hallway, Ben still at my side, and then down the main hallway. There was no cover.

The hallway was huge and wide open. I looked back to see Derek behind us but still a distance away. More gunshots rang out as I tried to cover my head with one hand, my focus shaken as something heavy pulled me down. I looked behind me to see that Ben had been shot at least three times.

"He's dead," The Female voice said

"No! No!!" I screamed at Ben, then at Derek, who was still just standing at the end of the hallway. "Ben! Please! Wake up! Please!" I started to shake him. I kneeled by his side and realized he really was dead. I looked up once more at Derek, lifted myself up, and continued to run. Derek was laughing; it was echoing through the hallway. He was still shooting at me as I ran. I ran up another staircase. I tripped on four football players that were lying dead on the stairs. They all had multiple gunshot wounds.

I tried to work my way up the stairs, but I started to slip on blood. I grabbed the railing on the staircase, trying to drag myself up. I reached the top of the stairs. I looked down to see that Derek was at the bottom. He was holding two guns in his hands. He looked up and smiled. I looked both ways, ran down a hallway with no cover. I sprinted as fast as I could; I saw at least five more bodies lying dead. I looked up to see the girl's restroom. I looked back to see that Derek had reached the top of the staircase. He shot at me once more, but it hit the wall beside me.

I quickly went into the girl's restroom. Surprisingly, it had a lock on the inside. I locked it, then turned to my left to see Lacy. Lacy was huddled down in the corner, covering her ears. I quickly ran over to her and shook her. Lacy screamed and started to fight until she realized it was me.

"Lacy! Lacy, it's me! Oh my God, I am so happy I found you!" I started to hug her.

"Everyone is dead, Jenn! Everyone is dead!" she sobbed.

"I know, Lacy, but we have to get out! We have to get out!" I tried to pick her up from the floor. Lacy continued to sob but eventually had the strength to stand up with my help.

There was no way out. Derek was outside that door. He saw me come in here, and he was not going to stop. Derek wanted me dead! He already explained it to me in detail. Derek had me in real-time, this reality, not my own.

Lacy struggled to stay standing. I could hear sirens in the background. The sound of help was getting closer, but something told me it was too late.

I heard three more gunshots against the door, and the lock had been burst open by bullets. Both Lacy and I hit the ground, covering our heads as we tried to catch our breath. I looked over to see that the door was wide open, and I looked toward the broken door to see the black boots walking in.

"End of the line, Jennifer." The Male voice said.

Derek was standing over me with the barrel of the weapon, simply glaring. I stood up and was eye to eye with Derek. He did not say anything but continued to point the gun at me. His look was evil. His hair was covering his left eye and his right hand with a black-gloved finger on the trigger.

"I told you. You're going to die, Jennifer." The Male voice said.

I shook my head, then looked down at Lacy, who had collapsed back on the bathroom tile. I was terrified.

This was the end for me.

"I told you this would happen, whether you believed me or not," Derek said, still pointing the gun.

"Then shoot me. Kill me! You have me! There's no way out. You got what you wanted, so kill me!" I shouted at Derek, who just stood there and tilted his head to one side. "I told you to kill me a while ago, and you know it! When we were at the park, and you told me I was already dead!"

I looked down to see Lacy looking at me with disbelief and terror in her eyes. I then turned my eyes back to Derek, and he said nothing. He then turned the gun towards Lacy and shot her four times. The complete terror had left her. I kneeled down beside her and started to scream. Lacy was dead.

"You fucking bastard! No! No!!!!" I screamed a blood-curdling scream.

Derek showed no emotion as he stood in silence. I was in shock and terror, crying and sobbing. Derek was still standing over me and then started to move closer. I gathered as much strength as I could to stand up. I tried to wipe away the tears in my eyes as best as I could.

"It was supposed to be me! Why didn't you kill me? You wanted me dead! You told me that!" I continued to sob.

"I never wanted you dead," he replied as he turned the handgun that he had and pointed it to his head.

"No! No! Please no!! Stop!!" I screamed.

The final gunshot rang out, quickly deafening me in the heat of the moment. Derek's body silently hit the floor. I fell to the floor, looked up, and screamed. I was sitting in Lacy and Derek's blood. I could not move; my body was paralyzed. I was not able to speak or scream. I sat there leaning against the bathroom wall panting and crying. I was in a nightmare and could not get out. There was no way out.

CHAPTER 23
ACTUAL REALITY

I sat in the principal's office with Ben. I watched as Principal Vaughn picked up the phone. I shook my head, trying to ignore the overwhelming voices and hallucinations. There was so much pain, sorrow, and suffering. Principal Vaughn and Ben only stared at me, wondering what I was doing.

"Yes, this is Principal Vaughn; I need you to put the school on lockdown," as he held the phone close to his face, his hand was shaking. "Yes, and I need you to get ahold of Derek Kretin's parents right away. Thank you," he set the phone back down. He then looked at me. "I hope your right about this, Jennifer," he said with concern.

"Yeah, I hope your right, Jennifer." Said The Male voice.

"I am. I know I am," was all I could say back as I looked at Principal Vaughn, then back at Ben.

I leaned back in my chair and gave a sigh of relief.

Ben sat beside me and continued to stare at me in shock. I looked right back at him with a straight face. I looked down to see that my hands were shaky and clammy. I felt like I was going to be sick. I started to get up from my chair, and Ben stood up too.

"Wait! Where do you think you're going?" asked Principal Vaughn. "You two are not leaving this room."

"I'll be right back. I have to use the bathroom," I said, holding the door handle. Principal Vaughn's phone rang, and he went into his office, and I could hear that he was now talking to the police.

I quickly made my way out of the office with Ben at my side. I headed to the main entrance of the school. I looked up at the clock, 8:20. *It should have started by now.* I walked down the staircase that led to the cafeteria. There was a massive window that looked out to the student parking lot. Police car after police car began arriving. I walked into the cafeteria and closer to the window. I looked toward the path that led to the pavilion.

Derek Kretin was walking towards the school carrying a large bag. Derek was wearing what I knew he would be wearing. A black jacket, jeans, black gloves, and black combat boots. I looked back to my left to see that the police could not see him approaching. I started to go outside and get the police officer's attention but felt a pull on my arm.

"No, Jenn! Do not go out there!" as Ben pulled me back. "He's going to kill you," Ben said, looking directly into my eyes.

"He's going to kill a lot more people if I don't," I replied as I pulled my arm away and pushed open the door.

I hurried outside and ran toward the police cars. The police watched me as I sprinted towards them.

"He's right there! Over there!" as I pointed to another side of the parking lot.

Just then, the gunshots began to ring out over the calm silence of the morning air. I quickly dropped down, and a police officer grabbed me and threw me behind his car.

"He's going to get you, Jennifer," The Female voice said as I shook my head.

I then looked up from the police car and saw Lacy walking toward the school cafeteria entrance through the parking lot. Lacy had no idea what was going on. I looked to see where Derek was, and he was parallel to Lacy and two other students making their way up to the school entrance.

"Lacy! Lacy!" I screamed and stood up from behind the police car. She looked in my direction. "Get down!" The police officer grabbed me once more and threw me behind his vehicle. My back was turned to Lacy. I stayed behind the police car and heard the officers firing back at Derek.

I got up once more to look for Lacy; she was on the ground. I tried to start running towards her, but another police officer grabbed me and kept me from going to her. I looked up again, trying to break the officer's grip, and saw two other students also down on the ground, and they had been shot by Derek.

I tried to get up one more time and break the officer's grip and run to Lacy.

"He's not going to kill me! Let me go!" I screamed at the officer, trying to pull my arm away.

I heard five bullets hit the police car we were standing behind. Both the officer and I hit the ground. Derek kept shooting at the officers, which was delaying them from firing him back. The gunshots finally came to a stop. I looked up to see that Derek was reloading his assault rifle. He dropped the rifle and started firing a handgun. He kept aiming toward the police car that I was hiding behind. More police cars began to arrive. They started getting out of their patrol cars and surrounding Derek.

"Drop it! Drop your weapon!" All of the officers' voices overlapped each other.

"Put the gun down now!" another officer screamed at Derek.

"Drop it! Drop it!" more officers screamed at Derek.

I stood up from the police car, frozen. There was nothing I could do. Derek then looked in my direction, still holding the gun in his hand. Derek then raised the gun to his head. I closed my eyes and covered my ears, and then heard the muffled gunshot.

I opened my eyes to see that Derek was on the ground from a self-inflicted gunshot wound. I fell to the ground, as I couldn't hold myself up anymore.

Firetrucks and ambulances came rushing into the parking lot. The officers were pointing at the three people down on the ground in the parking lot. They were trying to assist the firefighters and paramedics. I leaned up against the police car, still unable to hold myself up. I watched the first responders attend to Lacy as two more ambulances drove toward the other two students.

The last ambulance came for Derek as I saw the three ambulances go out of the parking lot with lights and sirens. The paramedics of the fourth ambulance covered Derek with a sheet. It was now controlled chaos. I was still sitting on the ground, leaning on the police car as tears came down my face. I saw a hand cross into my line of sight and looked up to see a police officer. I took his hand and tried to stand up. He helped me to my feet.

"Are you okay? Are you hurt?" asked the officer.

I just shook my head. I watched as police officers started marking off the school grounds with crime scene tape. Soon after, the media arrived. I sat halfway on the hood of the officer's car and watched everyone try to maintain control of the scene.

CHAPTER 24
ACCEPTANCE

I later found out that two students were killed that fateful day. Lacy had survived, miraculously. I did not know the two students that were killed. Nobody deserved to die, especially like that. I learned how much worse it could have been because I saw it. The funerals were aired on TV. Their names were Tyler Feldman and Kyle Becker, and they were only sixteen years old. The shooting made national news and flooded every news channel, and I cannot say that I was surprised.

I eventually went to visit Lacy in the hospital. They started allowing friend visitors as soon as she was stable enough. I will never forget what Lacy had said to me the first day I went to visit her. Lacy was lying in the hospital bed when she saw me enter the room. Her room was filled with flowers and balloons from all kinds of people from school and family. As soon as I looked at Lacy, she smiled at me, and I just smiled right back as I was wiping tears away from my eyes.

"Hey Jenn, it's good to see you," she smiled at me.

"I'm so glad you're going to be okay," I gave her a light hug and sat down in the chair beside her. "Listen, Jenn, you have a beautiful curse. Your mind works so much differently than anyone else, and you should be proud of that. You were able to conquer the hallucinations, delusions and save lives because of it," she held my hand. "You were able to go from your reality to actual reality to do what needed to be done. You knew what was going to happen, even though it wasn't real. You chose to stop it, and you did."

"Lacy, I didn't save everyone. Two people still died," I continued to cry.

"I'm sorry that I tried to stop you from not taking your medication. I just didn't want to see you go into that place again. It was scary for me to see you like that, and I didn't know how to help you," Lacy continued. "Your family didn't know how to help you, Jenn."

"It's okay. Lacy, it's fine, please don't worry about it. You have enough to worry about right now," I interrupted.

"Well, whether you want to believe it or not, your brain, or whatever is going on in your mind, saved a lot of people. You dared to tell someone about it, not knowing if it was real or not," Lacy began to sit up in the bed. "You chose to act against the evil plaguing your mind and life," Lacy sat there with both her hands on her lap.

I continued to look at Lacy with tears in my eyes. I did not need nor wanted recognition for what I had supposedly done. When I got back on my medication, it would not be my reality anymore. This tragedy would soon turn into a very distant memory. It would be flashbacks of what could have been a much greater tragedy. This was how life was meant to be.

I had to go back and live in the real world. For the first time, I was able to distinguish my reality and actual reality. It would not last long. I could only live in one, even if I genuinely wanted to be a part of this world. I hugged Lacy goodbye and told her to get well soon.

"I will see you soon, Lacy, and everything will be back to normal," I said as I turned away to walk out of the room.

I walked down the hospital hallways in what felt like slow motion. The light of the sun was drawing closer to the entrance of the main lobby. I was out of the hospital, looking forward to the walk home. When I got outside, I looked around to see all the leaves on the trees were going from dark green to orange, red, and yellow. Fall is my favorite season, but now it holds a very dim memory in my heart. Fall is now symbolic of a tragedy. People only saw a fraction of what a tragedy looks like.

Unfortunately, I witnessed it all. I saw some of the leaves falling off the trees, freely blowing in the wind. I looked around to see all the fall decorations that were surrounding the hospital lobby. The breeze was chilly when I went out the door, but the sun was shining; it was missing for a long time. I started to walk home, but I knew the one path I would not take home and the place I did not want to see. At least for now.

My name is Jennifer Bailey, I am fifteen years old, and I am schizophrenic. It is difficult for me to distinguish between my reality and actual reality. I was born with a curse, a beautiful curse.

"It's time to go home, Jenn," The Female voice said.

"Yeah, it's time to go home," I answered and smiled as I walked.

ABOUT THE AUTHOR

Nat NW offers a unique perspective in the world thanks to her career as a police dispatcher with paranormal gifts. By providing her insights into various cases with groups all over the United States, Nat is a quickly rising star in the paranormal field. She is becoming a name to call when you need an extra set of eyes when the strange comes knocking. Drawing inspiration from the stories she encounters from her work and her own experiences, Nat wrote this tale to help raise awareness for two of the most significant troubles facing American youth; mental illness and school shootings. Controversial as these subjects may be, all sides of the arguments can agree they are nonetheless important.